"Jess, don't yo **lock a door against me again!"**

Damien looked fed up. "I just don't understand you. Why did you change toward me so suddenly?"

Jessica shook her head. "I wanted out, so I got out. I don't want your no-strings relationship anymore, Damien. And whether you actually marry someone else or not doesn't even matter now."

He turned and pointed a finger at her accusingly. "You still want *me*! I could take you right now."

Something flared up ominously in her eyes. "What kind of triumph would that be?"

Damien turned as if he was unable to bear what he had just heard. He paused by the ruined door before leaving and said quietly, "This is no way to end a relationship."

He would never know how close she came to giving in to her uncontrollable emotions.

Books by Amanda Carpenter

HARLEQUIN PRESENTS
703—THE WALL
735—THE GREAT ESCAPE
759—RAGING PASSION

HARLEQUIN ROMANCE
2605—A DEEPER DIMENSION
2648—A DAMAGED TRUST

These books may be available at your local bookseller.

Don't miss any of our special offers. Write to us at the
following address for information on our newest releases.

Harlequin Reader Service
P.O. Box 52040, Phoenix, AZ   85072-2040
Canadian address: P.O. Box 2800, Postal Station A,
5170 Yonge St., Willowdale, Ont.   M2N 6J3

AMANDA CARPENTER

raging passion

Harlequin Books

TORONTO • NEW YORK • LONDON
AMSTERDAM • PARIS • SYDNEY • HAMBURG
STOCKHOLM • ATHENS • TOKYO • MILAN

Harlequin Presents first edition February 1985
ISBN 0-373-10759-5

Original hardcover edition published in 1984
by Mills & Boon Limited under the title *Rage*

CHAPTER ONE

THE scene should have been idyllic. The beautiful woman seated directly across from the distinquished-looking man at the small table had her chair pulled around for the best view from the French-style windows that led on to a tiny balcony. From the balcony one could look out over New York's most expensive and exclusive neighbourhood and over the far off and yet clearly visible nucleus of shops on Fifth Avenue. The view was dizzying, moving, ever-changing. At the moment rain was remorselessly drumming against the balcony's concrete floor, and the aspect outside was grey, dismal.

Inside, however, was a totally different story, for the living room which the two were occupying was spacious, the roof arching overhead, the muted colours in the decor rich in their subtle hues. The woman lifted an exquisitely hand-crafted silver teapot in one elegant hand with a look of enquiry to the man opposite her. Everything—the woman, the penthouse apartment, the expensive and tasteful original oil paintings strategically positioned—all suggested a restrained opulence, an unerring elegance, and an occasional, surprising slash of dramatisation.

The woman was as flawless and as perfectly groomed as the beautiful, shadowed room behind her. In the muted elegance of the room she stood out in a vivid splash of colour, and the man's eyes returned to her again and again. She was indeed the focal point of the room. Her winged dark brows were arched slightly at her companion. She was strikingly lovely, both at a distance and close up. Deep, dark red hair, wholly natural, was swept back from her slender shoulders and fell like a pure silken waterfall from her classical face. Her complexion was white, not a sickly pale shade of white, but a pearly, glowing ivory. The outline of her face was oval, excepting the twin jutting angles of high cheekbones and the startling surprise in an already startlingly pure visage were her eyes, for they were a strange, fascinating yellowish gold, cat-like in their shape.

The scene should have been idyllic, as the man nodded in response to the woman's unspoken question and she poured tea into his cup, but under the physical perfection of the attractive atmosphere the man sensed dark shadows that were not caused by the darkened sky outside, but by the emotions of the woman across from him.

Jessica regarded Justin with amusement and affection. He was somewhere in his early forties, his closely cropped blond hair fading to grey at the temples, and his blue eyes beginning to fan in lines at the corners. Nevertheless, he was extremely good looking, with a firm square jaw and a cleft chin, and a trim body that towered over six feet. Tall as Jessica was, she came only to his chin, even in her highest heels. Justin's eyes were keen and blade-bright. He rarely missed much with those eyes. As the thought flickered across her mind, her eyes clouded over to become carefully blank, expressionless. She wasn't sure she wanted him to read her that well, today.

She should have married him when she had the chance, four years ago. But that time was past and they both knew it. She'd felt something for him romantically quite a while ago, but it had been infatuation and hadn't lasted. He was a wonderful man and had been her loyal friend for coming up to ten years now. They knew each other very well. She had to smile when she thought back at how they had met. Justin, now a newly appointed judge, had been a young lawyer at the time and she had been just eighteen, fresh to New York from high school and Vermont. He had been a public defender and had been assigned to the group of anti-nuclear demonstrators who had got slightly out of hand, that she had been a part of. Something about her had attracted him and they'd become fast friends in a relationship that was to span many years.

She glanced outside and sighed. The rain kept coming down. It would rain for days, she was sure of it. And as she looked outside, she wasn't sure if it was the rain she sighed for, or herself. She was such a different person than that girl of ten years ago. She had to shake her head when she looked back at how her life had been. She'd climbed the ladder of success in the modelling profession until now she was widely recognised and acknowledged as one of the highest-paid and well-known models in the business. Success in capital letters, she thought. Her mouth twisted.

'You've the oddest expression on your face, my dear. Whatever are you thinking about?' As she looked at Justin, she noted the gentle, friendly concern on his face.

Her lips twisted into a smile again, but it was merely a movement of physical muscles and not a real smile at all. 'Nothing at all,' she said lightly, raising her cup to sip from it delicately. The cup was hand-painted bone china and she leaned forward to prop her elbows on the table. Her fingernails were painted a deep bronze and a sapphire ring winked on her right hand.

'You, my dear, are lying through your perfect white

teeth and we both know it,' he told her bluntly. 'I've known you too long and too well. Don't you think I could sense that something was wrong the moment I walked in that door?'

'What a terrible day it is outside!' she said with a sudden viciousness. 'I hate rain; I always gloom about the apartment, moping horribly, putting lines on my face and being a bitch. It must be menopause.'

She sensed him jerking with surprise and then he was laughing at her. 'The awful things you manage to come up with! All of twenty-seven, aren't you?'

She sipped tea, eyes down. 'Twenty-eight, but don't start counting, will you? So hateful to be reminded. . . .' Twenty-eight. Perhaps, if she was lucky, she had seven years left of her present career. Then the lines, those inevitable signs of ageing, would come. Oh, she had money enough, but the boredom! And, she admitted reluctantly, the possible rejection. . . . '. . . tell me,' she asked, in an effort to stop her flow of thought, 'are you going to the Trevors' engagement party tonight? I hear it is to be quite a social event.' Her voice as she said that last part was dry.

He smiled. 'That depends. Will Damien be there?' Rain pattered down endlessly from a lowering, sullen sky.

She watched the cascade with a mild look of distaste. 'If that infernal rain doesn't quit, I do believe I'm going to be flooded, even though I'm twenty-five storeys up! Just look at that balcony, will you?' She caught sight of his patient, knowledgeable eyes and sighed. It was no use prevaricating with Justin. Ten years is a long time to know someone and he knew her too well. 'Darling, Damien is Damien, and by definition is completely unpredictable from one moment to the next. I have no idea if he plans to go or not.' Her gaze shifted away from his and back again, piercingly. 'He's unpredictable, except perhaps that he quite hates the sight of you and any mention of you. Puzzling.'

'Not so puzzling. He dislikes our friendship and would love to make sure that I never set eyes on you again. Jealousy, Jessica, that green-eyed monster. He is a very possessive man, and that's why I'm wondering just a little at your unexpected invitation to me today. You've always gone out of your way to keep peace and distance between Damien and myself, and I believe that this is only the second time I've been in this apartment. Are you being careless, or reckless, darling?'

Her eyes shot to his and something flared in them before it was extinquished, like a candle being blown out. 'You see too much,' she murmured as she clasped her hands rigidly together, below his line of sight. 'Just be sure that Damien doesn't come between us, Justin Marsh. I value you too highly as a friend, and in fact am quite convinced that ours is the most ideal relationship of all. It's supportive, trusting and mutually affectionate, unclouded by nasty sex.' Her deliberate attempt at audacity earned her another laugh.

'But there is a great deal to be said for sex. . . .' Justin's eyes travelled down her figure appreciatively. Very tall and willowy graceful, Jessica nevertheless had a slight, suggestive curve to her breasts and hips that hinted at the sensuality in her lower lip. 'You know that Damien, for all his power and ambition, has no earthly claim on me. It makes him angry. He'd love to be able to order me to stay away from you and he can't. It's very frustrating for a man unused to opposition. No, my dear, he simply has to come to terms with the fact that you and I are fast friends and will always remain so, for you know I adore you. How is that devil, anyway?'

'The same as always, which is to say, different from day to day. When he is around, that is. Last week he was off to France and has only just returned.' She had herself well in control, proud of her unruffled voice, her serene expression.

Justin was not fooled and his hand tightened into a fist on the table. 'He's a bastard to treat you like he does! I'll bet he didn't even inform you of his departure as usual, carelessly leaving a scrawled note if you're lucky, not telling you when or if he'd be back! I can't stand the way he treats you!'

Neither can I, she thought, and closed her eyes, aghast at how she had nearly said it aloud. She made an effort, opened her eyes, and tried to speak calmly. It came out slightly ragged. 'You know that Damien and I started our relationship strictly on a no-strings basis. If I were to throw a childish fit and demand to know his every move, he would suffocate and I'd only be driving him away from me. As it is, he leaves for a time, but always eventually comes back. It's something I have to accept if I want to have a relationship with him.' She smiled mockingly. 'And what I feel cannot compare with the pain that I must make you feel. If I had any unselfishness at all, I'd send you out that door and tell you to never come back. I value your friendship so highly that I cause you pain.'

This time it was his turn to smile and his fingers reached out to pat her on the cheek. 'You know I appreciate our friendship above all things. I would marry you in a minute if you would have me and you know it. But as it happens, I want your friendship too much to spoil everything by my masculine pride and injured ego! You don't hurt me, you only bring me happiness. I just wish that Damien would give you the happiness that you deserve.' Under his gentle touch, she jerked, her composure cracking slightly. Justin stared at her, worried. 'You know that you aren't happy,' he said abruptly. 'And it's that scoundrel, I'll bet. What's he done this time? You can't hide from me that you're upset about something, for all you try. What's happened now?'

She brooded, stirring her tea endlessly, around and around. 'Damien's a troubled man. And who knows him very deeply. I don't, and would be the first to admit it. I don't know his compulsions. He never talks about himself or his past—oh, the superficial things, I know, but never anything revealingly. Black hair, black eyes, black murky shadowed past. He's driven. He never slows down, never lets up on himself, and never quits until he has what he wants. And he's good. He beats them in business, very fairly. Even you admit that. He's a brilliant man and I love him, but as for knowing him? Well, who knows Damien, after all?'

Justin stared at her. She looked very composed, madonna-like, pure. She returned his gaze unfalteringly, golden eyes glowing against white skin, hair aflame against the muted background of the room behind her. 'I regret,' he murmured, 'ever teaching you the art of evasion, though you should know as a former lawyer, I could not help but notice it. 'Fess up, my dear. What has he done?'

'Done?' she replied, splaying out her slender hands and looking over her nails carefully. 'Damien has taken into his head the notion that he must marry, that's all. He has yet to do anything about it, though.'

Her rueful gaze lifted to meet Justin's. His face had darkened angrily at her words. 'Marry! And who, pray tell, is he contemplating marriage with? Surely you?'

A light silvery tinkle of laughter, unamused, jarred on both of their nerves. She quieted quickly and said,

'Really, my dear, I expected more sophistication from you, of all people. One doesn't marry one's mistress. One finds a dull, suitable wife and then plays around. Quite a lingering fashion, though I must say I always felt so sorry for the mouse of a wife that had to stay at home, breeding like a cow, never having any fun.' She abruptly dropped her pose and leaned against one hand tiredly, something stark in her eyes. 'No, darling, Damien would never marry me. Unsuitable family background, no ties or money—he'll marry in the business, if I'm not mistaken.'

The blond man across from her was watching her with a strange, sad expression on his rather stern face. 'Jessica, Jessica,' he said with a queer moan. 'I've known you so long, and in the past three years you've changed almost beyond recognition. Where is that girl who told me so tempestuously that she'd never marry without love? Where is the girl who had stars in her eyes and a wonderful, simplistic way of looking at life and her ideals? Where is the girl whose flamingly explosive temper used to ignite almost instantaneously, at any given moment? Jessica, where did that splendid creature go?'

She regarded him wryly, with a small shake of her shapely head. Something in his words touched a part of her that quivered in response, but for the most part she was in disagreement with him. Once she had been that person he had described, but he didn't see the entirety of that past girl. He preferred to remember the good and forget the bad, and that was always a dangerous thing to do with the past. She'd once been every bit as tempestuous and explosive as Justin had described, but it was an unprincipled sort of high-spiritedness that had caused many problems. Along with the impetuosity had come a bit of indiscretion and along with the glorious red hair a vile temper. And the simplistic way of looking at life had never had a chance. One can't exist in this world, she thought, with a simplistic view of life. It can't be done, the world is too complex, too tangled and demanding. Black and white are good for ideals and religion, but people are varying shades of grey and even the most saintly have the dirt of sin on their hands.

She would never go back to what she had been before. That extreme youthfulness had been too uncomfortable. She was older and more experienced now, and more in control. She no longer flew off the handle at everything that went wrong. She was a pure professional at her job, hard working, conscientious and dedicated, and it had got her a sterling reputation which was highly respected. She wouldn't deliberately throw that away, and it had all been learned and earned with the control of her temper and that gloss and public poise that was both legendary and envied.

'I grew up, Justin,' she said quietly. 'I'm not that rash, brash child anymore and I'm glad of that. Some things in me will never change. You know that I will always abhor the thought of a nuclear war—who in their right mind wouldn't? But I no longer march in the streets, I talk to diplomats and Senators. The mood is constant but the method is perhaps more subtle. I love Damien, and he's the only man I would consider marriage with. In that way I will never change, and so I suppose I will never marry. I must be content with what he will give me, and I must not take the chance of destroying what little I've got of him by some stupid, ill-considered, thoughtless show of temper. I am in control of myself.'

Justin looked at her hands as they moulded the teacup lovingly. They were truly beautiful hands, slender, fragile-looking, feminine. They had once held a crudely painted protest sign and had once beaten a wall in an orgy of pure fury. He sighed. 'Jessica, I knew you. Sure, some things might have changed in you, but I know that with that great gorgeous mass of flame that crowns your head, a similar flame lurks in your heart. You have the devil's own temper, and you once gave back to Damien every bit of temper that he dished out. God, the vibrations of your clashes would make every building within a block tremble! Your temper and personality was probably what attracted him to you in the first place.'

She heard Justin's words but couldn't let herself react to them. Too much was at stake—all of her happiness, to be exact. She was so insecure in her relationship with Damien, everything so tenuous and transient. She couldn't let herself do something that she might regret. Though their relationship was based on no ties, like she'd told Justin, Damien would go away for a month or two at a time, but he would always come back to her, appearing on the doorstep like magic to stay for a while. And because she loved him, she never said no. She'd never had the chance to say no in the first place, had lost the struggle before it had begun and had lost her heart as easily. Three years ago, Damien had literally crashed into her life by sliding on a patch of ice on the pavement and knocking her down, and as much as she was then exposed to the world and fast acquiring the gloss of what was now her present image of sophistication, she had still been stunned with the overwhelming impact he'd had on her. *Wham!* and there he was, sleek and black-haired, drawling and urbane. He was so very handsome, it still made her heartstrings jerk just to look at him, his face very strong and evenly featured. He, too, stood tall, and she came only to his shoulder, which made her feel fragile and feminine. His whole body had a certain fluid, tightly knit, prowling grace that more than once reminded her of a stalking, slinking panther. He was the most exciting man she'd ever met. And if he walked out of her life, she would cease to exist inside.

But now Damien said that he thought he might make a marriage of convenience, in order to solidify some business matter—what, she couldn't remember—and that the marriage would not impair his freedom in any way. His freedom was so important to him.

She was about to become what was so quaintly termed 'the other woman'. It couldn't be borne. Jessica's very deep pride, even apart from her morality, would never let her continue her present relationship with Damien if he were to marry. Everything would come to a halt, and she would never see him again, and then she would die. She was mortally afraid.

Aware of Justin's scrutiny, she let nothing show on her face; no sign of emotion or distress marred the smooth classic perfection of her exquisite profile. Justin had a strange sense of foreboding as he watched that moulded profile and slender, arched neck, the shadows lengthening behind them. The woman before him was not quite real. 'You hide things very well,' he complimented her, raising his teacup in salute.

'"All the world's a stage", my dear,' she returned imperturbably, dusting a flick of lint from her black skirt. 'And don't you let anyone tell you differently. We act and act and act. My image is one that's plastered all over numerous magazines, gossip columns, and billboards, and not one of those many, many people will ever know what really makes me tick. It's not me they buy, it's the image. What is quintessentially me could be housed in any type of flesh, fat, thin, old, young. The lips, the hair, the eyes, the nose . . . they are rather nice, aren't they? But what do they really matter?'

'Do you know what I think, Jessica?' he said suddenly, and the tone in his voice made her turn her head to look at him with sleepy eyes that hid a look of assessment.

'Frequently, my love, but not at the moment.'

'I think that you still have that deadly dangerous temper locked away somewhere inside you and you are repressing it, controlling it, not letting out the pressure of the violence of the emotion. I think that there is a lit, burning fuse somewhere in you that will one day find and come in contact with the keg of dynamite you've tried to hide so well. Where do you put your rage? Where has it gone, Jessica? You're more dangerous now than you were ever in your life because before you vented your temper in harmless ways. You have so many good qualities, my dear, so many marvellous, loving, giving qualities, but your temper when bottled up like it is now, is going to turn to venom. Some day you are going to lose that fantastic self-control and blow sky-high. And I think that with the detonation of that forceful rage, coming from the passionate personality you're trying so hard to repress, you're going to flatten everything around you within a three mile radius. And it makes me somehow pity Damien for all of the man's strength of mind and forcefulness. It makes me pity you sometimes too and I fear for you, yes, fear for you both.'

The rain kept coming down, and it kept coming and coming, seemingly with no end. It seemed that heaven was crying all the tears that Jessica would never allow herself to cry. The rain was so depressing and, in New York City, had never seemed very clean to her. She sat there, like the perfection of a Michelangelo statue as she looked out the window at the rain, and Justin felt a thrill of pure aesthetic pleasure from just watching the wonderful symmetry of her sensuous body. Her composure was intact throughout his piercing observations, her face calm, untroubled. The purity of her red hair flowed down her graceful neck like an oriental silk and her brows winged across her forehead uncreased. But he looked into her eyes and felt the first real tremor of a deep unease that spread to a real fear.

In her golden eyes, something smouldered.

CHAPTER TWO

WHEN the front door opened much later and Damien walked in, Jessica was ready for him. She came forward smoothly, lips smiling a welcome and hands outstretched, and he stopped just inside the door to watch her approach. Then as she reached him, he took hold of her hands and pulled her against him for a long, lingering kiss.

She emerged from the embrace feeling slightly overwhelmed, and it was a familiar feeling for Damien always made her react that way. He just had to walk into a room for her to start tingling all over. She didn't even have to look around to see if he really was there; she always knew when he was near.

He filled up the living room with his vitality and power of personality, the long-legged, masculine body dominating the space, commanding attention. She let her eyes roam over the smooth straight line of his jaw, the heavy, satirical black brows, the sparkling dark eyes and the slightly arrogant hook to his strong nose. He meant so much to her, more than he really knew, for she was not one to tell of her love without being secure in the response. For all of her verbal reticence, however, she thought that he must surely know how she felt. She told him in so many ways, the warm glow in her golden eyes, the tender note in her voice when she spoke to him, the undemanding and yet unswerving attention she showed to him. It was, she felt, appallingly obvious.

'Ummn, you feel and smell marvellous,' he said in a husky murmur, the low tones of his caressing voice sending a thrill down her spine. She shivered at the delicious sensation. 'I need a drink.'

She sent a quicksilver glance over him. His business suit was immaculate and his hair as sleek as ever, but there was the unmistakable sign of tiredness written on his face. 'Go rest on the couch, darling. You'll find something waiting for you on the end table.'

He cocked an eyebrow at her. 'I'm convinced that you are a witch, woman, and that you read my mind . . . ah, brandy. Thank you.' He coiled up the length of his body and sat at one end of the couch, reaching for his brandy glass with one hand while loosening his tie with another. His hands were large and well moulded, the contours etching an impression of strength in one's mind. She folded herself as gracefully as he, and sank down beside him. He reached out and pulled her to him again, this time not for a kiss but just to fit her body's curves to his. She went willingly.

'Hard day,' she commented, eyeing him again with a gentle, almost concerned glance. She was concerned when Damien pushed himself too hard, which was most of the time, but she refused to let it show too much, believing that he would not want to be suffocated with feminine sympathy.

'Yes. I got a new secretary and fired her all in the same day,' he replied deeply, the satirical impression of his brows becoming more apparent since he wore a particularly forbidding look. Jessica was used to the expression, but she remembered for some odd reason Justin's remarks of that afternoon and realised that Damien to most people would seem quite devilish. They looked at his dark looks and his hostile moods and didn't bother to look underneath at the man who at times could be astonishingly compassionate. 'Damned incompetence. . . . She was so terrible, I called the employment agency that hired her for me and cursed at them for a full fifteen minutes. I get a new one on Monday.'

'Eating secretaries again, darling?' she murmured, a thread of laughter running through her pleasant voice. 'My, my. You should try your teeth on one of our younger secretaries. She looks particularly succulent, I believe that she might be to your taste.'

'Bitch as well as a witch, eh?' It was said with no malice in his voice, but rather a peculiar satisfaction. 'What are you cooking tonight, woman?'

'Droll, very droll.' She smiled at him and then disengaged herself to go to the antique drinks cabinet to pour herself a glass of wine. 'Actually, it's nearly time for me to start thinking of getting ready for Karen's engagement party. Had you forgotten it? Do you plan to go?' She had hoped that he would escort her, but he hadn't mentioned anything about it and she was always careful not to impose.

'Dammit!' he swore softly, and she turned with surprise to see his face tighten with annoyance. 'I had forgotten about it and I'm obligated to show up. I'm supposed to be taking Jake Coefield's daughter, Mary, and it's almost six now!'

She grew very pale at Damien's words, and her face became every bit as rigid as his, for a moment. Then it all just melted away as if the expression had never been and she looked at him mockingly, her eyes slanted wickedly and her mouth curved up. It was not an amused smile. 'Coefield's thinking of selling to you, isn't he? Is little Mary Mouse the one with whom you are contemplating marriage? Now that, darling,' and she raised her glass up to him rakishly, 'is droll indeed! How very amusing! Shall I introduce myself tonight?'

His dagger-keen glance sliced through her. 'Don't be

any more of a fool than you can help, Jessica,' was his biting remark. 'You should know better than that by now. I don't and never will love that girl, and I think it's a supreme mistake for a man to marry for love in the first place. However, marriage to Mary would be convenient. Her father likes me.'

She turned her back with the pretence of wandering to the spacious windows for a brief look out, but the real reason was so that she could hide her face and her hurt for a few minutes and get herself back in complete control. Damien had never pulled any punches with her. He had never lied to her and this was why she knew that when he told her that she was the woman he wanted most in the world, he was speaking the truth. That was also why she knew without a shadow of a doubt that what he said now was true. He was seriously thinking of marrying that unknown girl.

He was a devil, she thought agonisedly, gripping her slender wine glass so hard that it nearly broke and staring unseeingly out of the window. He was an uncaring, insensitive devil. 'Things could get to be a bit complicated, don't you think?' she said lightly, whirling gracefully from the outside view to encounter his brooding gaze. 'You would have to do quite a juggling act between all of your women.' She sounded as if she were enjoying the whole thing, like a huge joke.

'Not at all,' he responded crisply, though his eyes darkened with quick anger. 'You know the score and she would too. End of story.'

'Such a flat ending! Well, darling, I will bid you adieu for the moment, since I must shower and change for the party. Make sure the front door is locked behind you, hmmm?' She threw a quick, airy wave and started to stroll down the hall to the luxurious bathroom, sipping from her wine glass delicately. It was a good act.

The plush carpeting muffled the sound of his footsteps so she was unprepared for his hands descending heavily on her shoulders to turn her around. The wine glass was plucked from her fingers and deposited on the floor and then she was shoved up against the wall and he was bringing those firm sensual lips down hard on hers once more, grindingly, dominant. His hands held her still with a grip that hurt, and his powerful body trapped her fully. The kiss went on and on and towards the end she had her arms around his neck, kissing him back, and it changed for them both until it was a real caress. His black head lifted and he stared down at her with shuttered eyes, his gaze touching on her lush lips lingeringly.

'Well,' she murmured throatily, covering the hurt of his behaviour again with a look of amusement. 'If you want to kiss me, darling, next time just let me know. I'll put down my wine glass first.'

His mouth tightened ominously and his jaw flexed. When he spoke, it was with a silky, threatening tone of voice that made her feel cold. 'Don't be flippant with me again, Jessica. I'll see you later on tonight.'

She merely looked at him mockingly, one delicate brow raised in defiance. He flicked her cheek with a careless finger that hurt, and then he left.

As soon as the front door had closed behind him, her face changed, became sharper, hurt, vulnerable. She stared for a long time at the closed door with a miserable ache deep inside and suddenly the womanly sophistication dropped away and a lonely, frightened girl stood in the middle of the shadowed hall.

'Damn him! Damn him! Damn him!' she burst out, crying, and as quickly as it had come out, it stopped. She couldn't afford to ruin her complexion with tears before the party. Too many sharp eyes would be about.

An intense, frustrated fury welled up inside her and she whirled to stalk over to the phone, dialling jerkily and tapping her foot while she listened to it ring. In company she always was so controlled and contained, never making an unconscious move or an undisciplined one, but when she was alone she never could remain so held in.

She talked to Justin, instantly becoming cheerful and sounding unconcerned. She wondered, even as she spoke, why she bothered with the act. She was sure that Justin could sense and hear the hurt behind the bright chatter. After they agreed to meet in an hour, Justin more than willing to be her escort for the evening, Jessica replaced the phone receiver slowly. If a stranger were to look in on her at that moment, he would have found her expressions intriguing, as in about thirty seconds her facial features became cat-like, eyes narrowed and calculating, and then cynically amused, ending, finally, with an almost unbearable sadness.

Why, she asked herself silently, did she have to be such a fool over Damien? Why was he the one who made her heart race and her pulses pound? Why was he the one she wanted to hold her through the night, every night? Why, oh why couldn't she have fallen in love with Justin instead? She knew that he would make her a good husband if she ever could marry him. He would be faithful and caring, constantly supportive, and he would never hold her loss of virginity against her. He'd known almost from the start when she and Damien had become lovers and he had never spoken a word of recrimination or condemnation to her. He really understood her and that was a comforting thought.

But she couldn't imagine Justin in the same bed with her. The only person that she wanted to have by her, naked and loving, was Damien. She wanted Damien's devotion and husbandly care, his love and support and faithfulness. She wanted the one thing that he had once told her he was incapable of giving to any woman: his everlasting fidelity.

And once again, hopelessly, she wondered just what had happened to him to render him unable to give a husbandly devotion to one woman. The question would probably never be answered, she told herself with a brutal honesty.

She whirled and left the living room at a run. Enough time was wasted. She had things to do. She had to make herself so beautiful, so alluring, so sensationally sexy tonight that Damien would not be able to take his eyes off her. She would cast that other unknown woman in the shade. She would taunt him with what he would not have, because she would not be here tonight, waiting for him as she'd always done in the past.

She would fight for him and struggle to the very last, but as soon as those wedding vows were spoken it didn't matter if he never slept with his wife at all. He would most assuredly never sleep with her again. She would not give herself to him if he were married to someone else, for she would not make a mockery of that which she respected most of all and wanted more than anything: marriage. A fed-up look crept into her eyes as she thought of the possibility of him walking away from her. She wouldn't take him back. She would not countenance adultery. She had her pride.

But underneath that stiff pride something whispered, please, God, don't let him walk away from me now.

After preparing for the party with great thought and care, Jessica stood back from the mirror, gave herself a good long look, and started to laugh. A strikingly lovely woman posed in the mirror, bare leg angling out in a model's pose that was after years of practice quite naturally assumed. She was wearing a very little something in white, a filmy thin dress that looked and felt like a silk nightgown. It was cut slashingly deep between her breasts, just barely decent. It was fitted very tightly at the waist, immediately revealing to the experienced eye that it had been made especially to fit its owner. Then the dress flared at the hips in two gathered puckers, being pulled taut across her flat stomach and rounded buttocks, and the skirt was as wicked as the rest of the dress. Her long lean left leg was almost entirely bare as the wrap-around style skirt stopped a bit higher than mid thigh, but the other leg was nearly completely covered since the skirt angled dramatically down to stop at a point whose length just touched her right ankle. Every elegant, sensuous line of her body was either revealed by the clinging material so cleverly draped, or was completely bare. She didn't need to wear dresses designed to hide a physical flaw; Jessica dressed instead to adorn the lines of her body. At her tiny waist was buckled a rich, thick gold belt, with heavy gold bracelets clipped to her left ankle and her right arm and chunky gold earrings glinted through profuse red curls. Slim straps of leather, gold-toned, of course, complimented her graceful feet. The overall effect of her appearance was of a fascinating, barbaric sexiness so potent that long after she'd stopped laughing, a satisfied smile lurked around the edges of her perfect lips.

Golden eyes glowed with a vivid nervous excitement as Jessica's sense of playing with danger increased, charging through her like an electrical current. Damien would be enraged, absolutely livid. He was so unpredictable, she didn't know what he would do.

But that didn't matter. A stranger looking at her for the first time that night would never believe that she was the same woman that had only that afternoon worn a frightened, little-girl-lost expression. No one but she was even aware of that part of her personality. She was a sophisticated, worldly woman. She would not be hurt tonight, and she would not be vulnerable. No one was going to try to get close to the creature under the wonderful packaging. The wonderful packaging, again, would be the creature.

The doorbell rang and she went to answer it without surprise. Justin was well known by the night watchman downstairs and would be let right up. She stepped back and watched him come in, appreciation lighting her eyes. He looked very distinguished in his black evening suit and was a perfect foil for her own colouring and outfit. They would be one of the better looking couples at this huge extravaganza. A tiny thought crept into her mind and she dismissed it angrily, but not before ruefully acknowledging it as true. If Damien had escorted her tonight, they would have been without a doubt the handsomest couple there. She didn't want to think about him, though, or the coming evening. Her body jerked as she turned to hand Justin a glass of sherry.

'I've seen you in your "war paint" before, Jessica, and though I intellectually know how beautiful you are, it strikes me anew every time I see you like this,' he told her, shaking his head in simple admiration. 'Double torpedoes right at the son of a bitch, if I read my signals right. God, lady, what are you trying to do to all the other men at this engagement party tonight, send their blood pressure soaring sky high? That dress ought to be illegal.'

'Like it?' she asked mischievously, pivoting gracefully for his perusal. 'He's never seen it before. I think it'll do nicely enough, don't you?'

'Nice enough? There's nothing nice at all about that dress—what there is of it!' He tossed back his head to finish his drink. 'I know why you called me! You don't need an escort, you need a bodyguard. How'm I supposed to keep everyone from kidnapping you, right in plain sight? The bracelets are a nice touch. Just the right hint of erotic slave girl stuff. Shall I auction you off?'

She smiled again, but her heart was no longer in it. 'As long as I get to keep the profits. . . . Listen, Justin, I have another favour to ask of you and it's—well, it's an imposition, if you don't mind.'

'Well, come on, out with it. What do you need?' He smiled down at her and she felt a rush of affection for him that was quite platonic. He was always so good to her!

'Would you be my big brother?' she asked him, sighing deeply. 'You are so like the one I never had, the one I always wanted to run to when I got roughed up, the one I always wanted to fight my battles for me. Could I spend the night tonight at your house? Damien expects to come back here and I don't want to face him. If he marries her, I'm breaking the relationship. I won't be a part of that kind of set up. This is bad enough as it is, never knowing if he's just too tired to come over or if he's with someone else, never knowing if he'll still want me six months from now, never having any kind of security at all. Would you mind terribly if I slept on your couch?'

'My dear,' he murmured, reaching out to cup her cheek briefly. 'I'll be anything you want me to be. And yes, you can sleep at my house, though there's no need to resort to the couch as you know! I'll call my housekeeper right now to set up a room for you. The problem is, though, that this will solve things only for one night. You're welcome at my house for as long as you care to stay, but we both know you won't, will you?'

'No,' she said slowly, shaking her head. 'I won't. I'm going to have new locks put in the door tomorrow. I daren't do otherwise, after tonight. He's going to be livid!' She shuddered delicately, glancing up with contrition at Justin's handsome, dignified face. 'I'm asking a lot, I know. I'm sorry to be a burden to you.'

'You aren't a burden. You are a joy. And what else are friends and big brothers for, anyway?' he told her calmly, smiling. She got the strangest feeling that he was looking forward to Damien's wrath.

She also wondered if Justin was as in love with her as he had once claimed. Damien, claiming never to have been in love with a woman, was nevertheless going to be furious at the sight of his lover with a man he hated heartily. The one thing that gave her any kind of hope for the future was that she knew that Damien was not indifferent to her. Otherwise he would not have kept coming back to her for three years. Three years. That was longer than anyone else he'd seen, she knew. Justin, on the other hand, was perfectly happy to be her friend in the purest platonic way, and he never demanded anything else. She rather wondered if he was merely happy to be a part of her circle of friends. She knew that he thought she was as exotic as a movie star, though he would never admit it. She was a splash of gaiety in what was a very dignified and sober life. And, although she saw him clearly for just what he was, she still loved him and was deeply thankful for his unswerving friendship and support. And wasn't that also part of the definition of a friend? Her eyes went unfocused and she stared off into nothing for a moment as she realised how barren of support her life would be without Justin. She didn't feel that Damien offered her much support, and had to recognise that it was partly her own fault. She'd been too afraid to ask for it.

The unfocused look faded and she smiled brilliantly at Justin. 'Thank you. Let me get a few things together and then I'll be ready. Has it stopped raining?' She had pulled the curtains closed some time ago.

'Yes. The sky is still pretty grey, but it's finished raining, I think,' he replied, settling down for a wait.

She was quick, pulling only a change of clothes out of the closet and piling a few cosmetics into a bag. Then she draped a crushed velvet, full-length evening cape across her shoulders. It was a deep, royal purple, finishing off her whole ensemble majestically.

Taking a deep breath, she steadied her mind, thought calm nothings for a minute, and went out to face the ordeal.

The Trevors' house was more a mansion than a home, she thought, shuddering a little in the darkness of Justin's BMW as they pulled into the long drive. The whole huge architectural monstrosity was lit for Karen's engagement party. Karen was an only child, like Jessica, and her doting parents intended to send her off with as much of a bang as they could afford. Being quite wealthy, they could afford a lot. The party tonight was going to be for as many as three hundred guests and all of them would be high-class, high-powered, and highly sophisticated.

And then there would be, of course, Damien. Her jaw clenched as she felt a queer jerk in her stomach, sheer nervousness, that she couldn't control. She waited while Justin left the keys to the car with the parking attendant hired especially for the occasion, and they went up the wide, wide steps to the imposing double-front doors, pushing a button to their right. The solid dark oak swung open on silent hinges, and they entered into the light, spacious hall. Jessica's wrap was deferentially taken, and she caught a quick glimpse of the maid's wide, awestruck gaze as the rich cape fell from her nearly naked shoulders. A formally uniformed waiter just coming from the back of the hall with a loaded tray stared at her and nearly tripped. She hid a smile.

'Er, did I happen to tell you to "knock 'em dead"?' Justin murmured in her ear, laughing. He too had seen the waiter's comic reaction. 'Bang on, my dear.'

'Behave, you wretch,' she whispered out of the corner of her mouth, eyes dancing gleefully, 'or I'll stay at a motel tonight, for spite.'

'Never that. Come on, it's time to face the lion's roar.' He tucked her slender white hand into the crook of his arm and they both went forward.

She was so tense underneath the calm, perfect, passive face she presented to everyone, that when she looked casually around the room to find Damien she sagged slightly against Justin when she realised that he wasn't there yet. Justin patted her arm in understanding but did not have any time to say anything to her before they were swept into a large, laughing group of mutual acquaintances.

He took a drink for her from one of the trays carried by passing waiters and she sipped at that from time to time. It seemed to help. She spent her time talking animatedly or listening, apparently enthralled, to anything anyone had to say to her. She nodded to friends, acquaintances, and anyone who stared at her with admiration, ignoring the more obvious oglers, and inwardly she was sick at heart, a mass of miserable apprehension. And she knew. She knew just as soon as he stepped into the room. She felt him, felt the stares of people turning towards the doorway, heads lifting, attention shifting. Damien did that to people. He attracted attention like a magnet attracted iron, much as she did.

Slowly, insolently, ignoring the pounding of her heart and the dry, dull taste in her mouth, she turned on her heel, threw her head back with a convincing show of arrogance, and watched the small group of people just entering the huge ballroom. Her pose was deliberate, much like the pose she had observed in her bedroom mirror, one leg thrown out, bare and seductive. The light caught on the gold at her ears, arm, waist and leg as focus points and gleamed off ivory-smooth, healthily glowing skin. Though she stood very near to Justin, in her white dress she was somehow set apart, as if under a spotlight all by herself.

She stood and stared at the group of four. The two older people were obviously Mr and Mrs Coefield, so that left the younger girl as Mary, Damien's date. She stared and nearly laughed, and then nearly wept, as she looked at the face of a very young, very plain, very shy little mouse of a girl. She was wearing a dress of obvious cut and expense but it didn't seem to help the sloping shoulders, the thick waist and the dull quality of her skin. Damien was bending his head to her and being charming as only he knew how, she saw, and the mouse was responding with a fumbling eagerness. He gallantly gave her his arm, and she blushingly put a small hand on his sleeve, and the entire sight made Jessica want to throw her glass at him in an uncontrolled spasm of fury. She gritted her teeth at the pain and the anger of it all, and nearly jumped out of her skin when a hand touched her bare back.

'Calm down, my dear,' Justin's voice spoke right by her ear. 'You know that she can't hold a candle to you. If he had any sense at all he would be punching me in the jaw, forsaking every one of the Coefields, and dragging you home to make violent and passionate love to you, but then I always did say that Damien had little sense. Intelligence, yes, but damned little sense. He should have married you years ago.'

'Yes,' she spoke through her teeth, not caring if Justin saw through her façade to the anger pulsing underneath, and she missed the odd look that he gave her. 'That he should have, darling. That he should have.'

The hand at her back increased in pressure, gently. 'Offence is the best defence, my dear. Let's go and be introduced.'

Just at that very moment, she saw Damien's head lift up, the black hair catching and reflecting the overhead lights much as her own glossy mane did, and his eyes moved over the well-dressed crowd, alighting on her. By his sudden absolute stillness, she felt the shock go through him at the sight of her in the sensuous, provocative dress with Justin putting a proprietorial hand to her naked back. Suddenly the ordeal that she was expecting began to carry a flavour of delicious malice, and she found herself almost looking forward to what would be, if nothing else, an exhilarating clash. At that thought a shock of self-awareness ran through her. Justin had been right: she had at one time stood up to Damien and willingly threw back at him every bit of temper and fire that he dished out. It had been some time and it had been too long.

'Yes, darling,' she purred, smiling a very, very naughty smile. Justin chuckled at the sight and Damien, she saw, even from that distance, caught it. His reaction was not amusement, however, and she knew that under the urbane, charming man that stood conversing easily with several different people there was a growing wave of menace and fury.

They moved forward, were stopped several times by different acquaintances, and finally managed to approach the small, tightly grouped knot of people. Jessica saw Mrs Coefield look up, catch a glimpse of her, and betray an instant of startled dismay before quickly hiding it. Then she and Justin were upon them, and introductions were made all around as light, undemanding pleasantries were exchanged.

Catching another look from the older woman, she thought, that lady would like me dead. Is it because her precious daughter is hanging on to a very gorgeous and eligible man? Is she afraid that I might lure Damien away from Mary Mouse? If so, she doesn't know the half of it. What would everybody's reaction be if I simply stepped forward, smiled and said, 'Hello, so good to meet you all. I'm Jessica King, Damien's mistress, but don't let that bother anyone. He still wants to marry your mouse.' Shrieks, swoons and slaps. She put her empty glass on a tray and managed to take another off before the waiter disappeared into the crowd.

And of course she said nothing of the sort. She merely smiled winningly, shook hands with everyone, including Damien, felt his bone-crushing grip on her ringless hand and laughed at something Mr Coefield said. 'No, it was not poured over me out of a bottle, but it was especially made by a friend of mine,' she replied, glancing with brimming eyes down at herself. Standing next to Mary, a deliberate manoeuvre, she wasn't sure who was the obscene one: Mary Mouse for her atrocious choice of dress—nice, but wholly unsuited for her body's shortcomings—or herself for such glaringly obvious glowing good looks. Side by side, she mused, we must both seem obscene.

She glanced up sideways and saw that Damien was observing the differences between the two of them also. Then his eyes met hers, and she saw such a fierce molten volcanic eruption leaping out of those black eyes that she was briefly taken aback at the sight. It was frightening, to see that look out of a perfectly smooth, smiling urbane mask. She was sure that only Justin, herself, and Damien fully knew what was going on.

Everyone stood and made small talk, and Jessica knew that she joined in, but she hardly remembered what she said, and she knew it didn't really matter anyway. It was just surface noise, covering up a silent battle that she was waging with Damien.

Somewhere, out of sight to the left, music started up and she looked around at Justin's touch. 'Yes,' she murmured in response to his question and he lead her out to the dance floor. Once out, she shamelessly put her soft arms around his neck, letting her body be moulded close to his, and laughing silently up into his eyes as they barely made the excuse of a dance circle, looking to all observers like engrossed lovers. 'Is this how it's done, darling?' she asked innocently. 'Is he watching, by any chance? I daren't look.'

His head lifted briefly. 'Oh, yes,' he stated calmly. 'I wouldn't be surprised if he *did* come and knock me on the jaw in front of all these people. I'd do it. Jessica, you minx, stop that.'

'Is he dancing?'

'He's with your mouse.' She took a quick deep breath.

'She's sure as hell not mine!' That startled them both, for she had meant that breath as a temper-calming agent, not a means of venting petty spite. After the first moment of surprise, though, Justin looked thoughtful.

All he said was, 'So she's not, my dear. Pardon me.'

She wanted to apologise at that, but the pressures she was experiencing made her feel so tight, and explosive with anger that she didn't dare open her mouth. For the rest of the dance she concentrated on getting her tongue and her self back in control, unaware that both the man she was dancing with and the dark man across the dance floor were watching her very closely.

The dance ended all too soon, and she looked up at Justin as he whispered, 'Here he comes.' Feeling again that cowardly panic, she started to whisper back, but there he was, tapping Justin on the shoulder politely while looking murder into his eyes, and then Damien was asking her to dance.

She said with a deliberate, insolent flippancy that was a goading reminder of that afternoon, 'I don't know, do you, Justin? I believe I'll have to check my dance card, if you'll excuse me. . . .'

With a furious, abrupt movement, Damien grabbed her arm bruisingly and yanked her towards him as the first strains of another tune began. She could just imagine the raised eyebrows at that and asked him tauntingly, 'Have you told the Coefields yet the exact nature of our relationship, darling?'

'I will warn you only once, Jessica,' his quiet voice spoke volumes, and she sobered as she was scorched by the heat from those incensed eyes. 'I want you to go home alone, right now, alone. I will not have Marsh pawing you about in front of me, by God!' She nearly winced as the words, thrown like missiles, flayed at her already raw nerves. 'And you and I will discuss this later on tonight.'

'Will we?' she said strangely, but he didn't notice for he was too wrapped up in his own rage and reaction. His hands, to the casual observer, were resting lightly on her hips, but she felt the pain that he exerted as he gripped her so tightly. In all fairness, she knew that he was probably not even aware of what he did. 'Might I remind you, darling, that I go when and where I damn well please and with whom, just as you do, and I will not be ordered from the room like a five-year-old brat? There is, as you may recall, no ring on my left hand to restrain my actions.'

'Five-year-old brats,' he said softly, eyes glittering, 'in my book are spanked, not sent from the room, and I might add a warning to that, since you are not acting like an adult tonight and are reminding me more and more of a badly disciplined brat!'

'Oh, darling!' she pouted prettily, moving her hips against him sexily, though discreetly, 'is this really the body of a five-year-old brat? If so, you should be arrested for child molestation.'

'You bitch, you say the foulest things sometimes,' he hissed furiously and she shrugged.

'Only when pushed to it, Damien. And I warn you, don't push me too far.'

Their eyes clashed head on, and she felt dizzy from the impact of his forceful personality, but she had gone too far to back down now. Her pride had taken all the beating that it was going to, and she was beginning to fight back. He whispered commandingly, 'Go home.'

With an indifference that stemmed from hopelessness, she said, 'No.'

And at that, she had a strange impression, as her eyes no longer focused on Damien but instead turned inward. The turbulent emotions churning inside her were convoluting, coming together, fusing into something so powerful and frightening to her that she was taken aback at the force of the rage inside her. And she no longer wondered how she was going to handle Damien's anger. She became worried enough at how she would handle her own.

CHAPTER THREE

THE rest of the evening ended up being very much the ordeal that Jessica had anticipated. Mary Coefield announced later on that she was going to the ladies room, and Jessica had immediately stood to go with her, ignoring the warning stare from Damien. Accompanying the younger girl she soon found to her dismay that Mary was actually likeable, and she hadn't wanted to know that. The younger girl was shy and pathetically pleased with the attention that Damien had been showering upon her. 'For you know,' she confessed awkwardly, 'he's the type of man that I would have thought someone like you would go out with. I never dreamed that he would be interested in me.'

Oh, my dear Lord, Jessica thought, closing her eyes for a moment in deep pain at the artless, innocent words.

She had wanted to hate Mary and after talking with her briefly, she found that she just couldn't. And that made her anger towards Damien burn even brighter. For the rest of the evening she sat silently, smiling when spoken to but otherwise preoccupied with her thoughts. Damien asked her to dance one more time and as they circled the floor, drawing many admiring glances for the striking couple they made, she said to him lowly, 'Don't you hurt that child, Damien. I'm warning you. Don't you dare hurt her. She's too young and unsophisticated to understand the rules of the game you like to play.'

37

'What's this?' he asked mockingly, his low, deep voice reaching into her chest as he held her tightly against him. 'The mistress sympathising with the wife? It must be a novel situation, first one in mankind's memory. What did happen, when you so obviously followed her to the ladies room?'

But she had heard only one thing, and her world whirled crazily for a moment as shock coursed through her. 'You've already asked her, then?' she whispered through dry lips.

'No,' he replied after an apparent hesitation, and she shuddered briefly from relief, only to have her heart sink again as he said, 'Not yet.'

She spent a thoroughly miserable night at Justin's, listening to the bedside clock and the traffic noises and finally sleeping, though badly.

She declined Justin's offer to see her home and called a taxi first thing in the morning. She needed to get several things done, most importantly to see to new locks being put in her front door. She hated to imagine Damien's reaction to this. She hated to imagine his reaction to her disappearance last night. She hated herself sometimes, because she was always running away from an unpleasant situation, always being such a coward.

Still she really had no inkling as to what to expect as she quietly unlocked her apartment door early that morning. Flicking an impatient hand through her hair which sent it flowing about her shoulders in a glistening, eye-catching swoosh, she tiredly dragged her overnight case into the living room and then stopped abruptly. Her eyes widened in surprise as Damien's long form uncurled from a reclining position on the couch. They surveyed each other warily, silently, appraisingly, and she took in the deeper lines around his lean dark face, the blue-black shadow of unshaven beard on his jaw, and the rumpled glossy hair which was usually so neat and sleek.

'Good morning,' she murmured composedly, though inside her heart was beginning to race in uneven, slugging pounds.

'Is that all you have to say for yourself?' he came back quietly. For having been taken by surprise, he looked remarkably in control of the situation, with one eyebrow already up in that sarcastic sneer she hated so much and long, strong arms crossed over his chest.

'What else would you have me say?' she asked simply, putting down her purse and swinging around to head for the kitchen. 'I'm dying for a cup of coffee. Do you want some?'

Hurting hands clamped down on her slender shoulders and whirled her around to face him again. Now there was no mistaking the look of rage on his tired, drawn face, and she stared up at him, frightened. There was something else showing in his expression, but she didn't dare try to define it.

'Where were you?' he snarled, shaking her hard. 'Where were you, dammit?' He was bruising her shoulders and she struggled to get out of his grip.

'I don't really think you want to know that,' she came back swiftly, trying futilely to shove away his hands. She couldn't, and she knew that she wouldn't be able to when she had started. He was too strong for her to best him physically.

'Justin!' The word came out of him as if he had a bad taste in his mouth. He threw her from him and began to pace the large room like a caged animal. Then he whirled swiftly and began to throw words at her as if he were striking blows, and she turned her head as if to deflect the pain. 'Do you know what I thought last night? Do you want to know what my reasoning was? I thought that you and Marsh perhaps went to another party and you were delaying our discussion that was to have occurred last night. I thought you were being spiteful, trying to test my patience, and then you didn't come. Then I thought that there must have been an accident and you might be hurt, so I called every damned hospital in the telephone book because I was that worried about you! Worried, my God!' He stared at her from across the room, his eyes burning like live coals and his hands clenching and unclenching. 'Then,' he whispered, and it was like a scream of rage and pain, 'I called the police.'

'Damien,' she moaned, 'please stop. I didn't realise, I didn't——' Something seemed to stop her throat then, and she stared at him with huge, wounded eyes. Everything in the world seemed to be falling apart all around her and the craziest part about it, she thought dazedly, was that she hadn't even had warning when she got out of bed that morning. She wanted to tell him that she had not slept with Justin but merely spent the night in a spare bedroom in order to get away from him, but suddenly the years of jealousy that she had suffered and the uncertainties and loneliness all welled up. She looked at him and said nothing.

'Fool that I was,' he hissed through his teeth. 'I didn't actually realise what must have happened until it was around three or four in the morning, and then I realised that you wouldn't be coming back. And the rest of that sleepless night I thought of you in his arms. Jessica,' he said, almost gently, and the sound made her shudder violently, 'it's a good thing I didn't know where Marsh lives. Otherwise, I don't believe either of you would be alive to see this day.'

Something akin to hope was kindled inside her heart

at that, and she looked at him, nearly betraying her eagerness. He was jealous! He was actually jealous of Justin! He really cared! She took a hasty step forward, hand outstretched, only to jerk to a halt at his next words.

He had turned casually to the drinks cabinet and poured himself a brandy from what looked like a nearly empty carafe. When he turned back his saturnine face wore a mocking mask, and she knew that he had retreated into that part of himself which he would let no one else enter. 'Tell me, darling,' he drawled, drinking insolently, 'was he good?'

She stared at him, the eagerness dying out of her heart and her hand falling lifelessly to her side. She stood as one stricken mortally, his cruel taunt coursing through her like a bolt of electricity. Then her golden eyes darkened as something seemed to go *ping!* in her head, like a rubber band snapping or an iron bar breaking. Without conscious volition her left hand swept out, grasped a delicate porcelain antique vase and she flexed her arm spasmodically. One part of her stood back and admired with a cool objectivity her accuracy in aim and also his amazing agility for stepping swiftly out of the way. The vase smashed harmlessly against the wall behind where he had stood.

'Jessica!' he rapped out, and she didn't know who was more surprised at what she had done, Damien or herself, but she was too incensed to really care.

Suddenly sick to death of the careful perfection of the apartment that she had strived for so long to make beautiful, she whirled in a frenzy to grab at ornaments, flinging them not only at a stunned-looking Damien but at sterile, meticulously hung oil paintings and blank wall space. Her long loose red hair floated around her head like a demonic aureole, a flicker of volcanic fire, and her body swung from side to side, as tense as a tightly strung longbow.

He was very quick to move to her, jerking her arms down to her sides and shaking her roughly, hard, and she screamed at him furiously, 'Get out! Get out! Get out!'

His hand cracked against the side of her cheek imperiously. 'Snap out of it, Jessica!' he ordered tersely, 'you're being stupidly hyster——'

Her hand flashed out, as swift as his had been and cracked across his taut cheekbone with enough force to snap his head back, and his words were bitten off abruptly. His hard teeth came together in an audible snap and he stared down at her with eyes that seemed to be leaping right out at her with the force of his fury, his hands back to her shoulders, tightening until she felt sure that her collarbone would break.

'Who,' she spat at him, the delicate curve of her mouth disappearing into a snarl and eyes molten hot, 'gives you the right to strike at me, Mr Kent? Before God, you have gone too far! Now, I said get out! If I have to, I will scream at the top of my lungs, damn you!'

His left hand moved slowly to her neck and he rested it there thoughtfully for a moment. 'I've never come this close to doing you violence,' he whispered almost calmly, 'but I really think I could now.'

She did not feel a moment's fear for she was too far gone in her own rage for that. She didn't even have time to feel the hurt that she knew would come in the silence of her isolation. All she could feel was a welling tide of hurt and fury and everything that had been repressed for much too long, and the tide threatened to sweep her away with its strength.

'What do you want from me?' she screamed at him,

breaking away from his grip and hurtling to the other side of the room. 'In three years, in three hellish years, I still don't know what in God's name you want from me? Why do you keep coming back, damn you? Why do you tear me apart like this?'

He stood taut, with arms down by his sides and body entirely still, and only his glowing black, emotion-filled eyes and jerking jaw muscle portrayed that he was still alive. 'You know what I want from you,' he said, and the way he said it was an insult. 'I've never lied to you, you knew the score from the beginning. I never promised to give you more than I could give to you!'

'But you keep demanding more from me! Do you think I don't feel it? Why the hell should you expect fidelity from me when you don't give me yours? Why are you erecting a double standard for both of our actions? Why shouldn't I spend the night at Justin's? I have every earthly right! No strings, that's how it's supposed to be. You want me when you want me and you walk away afterwards, with never a thought as to what *I* feel or what *I* need!' She was sobbing from the force of the tidal wave that was sweeping her away, and her words were barely coming out loud enough for him to hear. He stood as though shocked to the core, and then he wasn't there anymore as her eyes filled with blinding tears. Not wanting him to see her crying, she turned her back and stared sightlessly out of the patio glass doors. 'I've needed you to be here sometimes, over the years when I've had no one to hold on to in the middle of the night, and you haven't been here! Well that's all fine and good, and I was managing to handle my own life all right, thank you, and now you have the almighty nerve to come here, take advantage of my hospitality—hah! There's a euphemism for you!—and tell me bedtime stories about the other woman you intend to marry! What the hell do you want to do, *see me bleed?*'

And the world shattered into a thousand tiny, glittering, tinkling pieces as she stared, horrified, at a growing stain of red that crept down her clenched hand. She had pushed her hand through the glass doors.

'Oh, my God!' With just a few steps, Damien was right there, his hands reaching urgently for hers and he was pulling a long wicked-looking piece of glass from her hand very carefully. She had time to notice that his long lean fingers were shaking as much as hers seemed to be, and then he was putting a gentle arm around her and urging her down the hall to the bathroom. She went, as the tide of rage washed over her and was gone, leaving her in a weak, shaking aftermath. When Damien pushed her down on the bathroom stool she complied dazedly, and when he carefully washed out the cut in her hand, she made no protest. He asked her abruptly, 'Where's the first aid kit?'

'In the hall closet, she whispered numbly. He went out of the room and was right back with the kit in his hands. He put antiseptic on the cut and silent, diamond-bright tears slipped out of her eyes to slide down the ivory of her cheeks. The tears looked so startling against the doll-like perfection of her skin that he stopped for a moment and was very still. She felt his stillness and looked up involuntarily and he looked like he was in such torment, in such racking pain that she stared back, golden eyes wide. Her uninjured hand crept out to him and then faltered back, as she remembered the time before when she had wanted to reach out to him, but this time his back wasn't to her and he saw the unrestrained, uncontrolled movement and caught his breath. Then his own hand was out, against her cheek, rubbing very tenderly the place where he had struck her earlier, wiping away the gleaming drops of wetness. 'No tears,' he murmured lowly. 'Oh, please, Jessie, no tears! I can't stand to see you cry, I can't stand the sight of those tears . . . but then, that's just another selfish part of me, isn't it, darling?'

He gathered her up into his strong, comforting arms and rocked her carefully back and forth while she let forth the deluge of tears she had refused to shed for so long, and for the first time in their relationship, she couldn't be strong. She curled her uninjured hand weakly into the front of his shirt, buried her bright head against him and just cried her heart out. She had crumpled and was showing Damien a totally new and unsuspected part of herself, a completely vulnerable, helpless side of her that he had never been privileged to see. She didn't even care that it was he she was crying with, for all she was aware of and needed was someone strong and warm to hold her close. He ran a soothing hand over her shuddering head and pressed soft lips against her cheek.

'Jessie,' he whispered after a while, 'please, darling, let me see your hand and finish wrapping it up. It will only take a minute. Just sit back. There, you'll be all right. I'll just take the gauze and wrap the cotton pad into place . . . there. I'm all done and now, you come back here, no, don't pull away! You come right back here and let me hold you close again. That's it. That's it, love. Hey, now you don't need to cry any more! Jessica, now, stop that . . . oh, Jessie.' He tilted her head up, took one look at her drowning eyes, and with a deep groan his head came down to block out the brightly glaring overhead bathroom light and his lips were on hers. She moaned, closed her eyes, and with a sudden fierce shudder, she reached up to wind her arms urgently around his neck.

The kiss was in its own way as violent as their earlier clash had been. For Jessica there was a quality of despair and hopelessness in her urgent, seeking hands, and she sensed that he was experiencing some kind of emotion that was akin to the fury he had felt for her before, but this emotion wasn't as destructive as the other had been. He wasn't trying to hurt her now. He was communicating his need for her with every eager, pressing caress from his large warm hands. She was out of control from the very beginning.

He picked her up and carried her to the bedroom to deposit her on the bed, not bothering to be gentle now and thrusting aside her clothes with a disregard for anything but his own desires, stripping her until she was naked. Then he took her and she nearly cried out how very much she loved him, but something held her back and troubled her mind, even as her body shook with the pleasure he was able to give her.

Afterwards, he asked her, still breathing hard from the urgency and passion of their lovemaking, 'Did he give you as much pleasure as I do, Jess? Did you enjoy him like you enjoy me? Answer me!'

She closed her eyes, felt such deep pain and despair at his words, and let none of it show on her face. Nothing had changed, not essentially. He still viewed their entire relationship from the sexual aspect, whereas she viewed their sexuality as a means of expressing her love for him. He was jealous, sure, but the jealousy was that of a canine hoarding a prized bone, not of wounded affection.

She forced herself to whisper quietly, 'No, Damien. Shh. Go to sleep.' And she felt him frowning at her, but refused to look at him and presently he did fall asleep, heavy arm thrown over her with a possessiveness that made her want to cry. His head was thrown back and the muscles of his neck were in strong relief. She rolled her head over and looked at the pulse beating in that strong column and wondered at the life that she loved so much and that could give her so much pain.

Though she was very tired, she didn't fall asleep. She lay in bed and watched Damien breathe, the hair-roughened chest rising and falling regularly, evenly. She ran her eyes over the long length of him time and time again, lovingly, sadly, and wondered where she would find the strength to do what she had to do.

She slipped out of bed later and made some coffee, carrying the silver tray into the living room and settling on to the couch. The excess of emotion from both last night and this morning had been too much to maintain. A feeling of passivity and calm washed over her, stemming from exhaustion, and the very lack of feeling was a comfort to her.

After a while a sound from the hallway made her turn her head calmly. Nothing could be gained from any more tears, and she had set her face with a resolve that came from that emotional exhaustion, so her face was calm. She was able to smile at Damien gently. She didn't want to hurt him. She had never wanted to hurt anyone. But she could not allow herself to be hurt anymore, either. 'Good morning,' she murmered, 'or should I say, good afternoon? Did you sleep well?'

'Yes.' He was shirtless and his black hair was still ruffled from sleep, but his dark eyes were alert and bright. He looked from her to the chaos scattered all over the living-room floor and had to laugh. His teeth were very white. 'Nothing seems to bother you sometimes! I've never seen anything quite like it— you're as calm and as serene as a Mother Superior and then, without warning or premonition, you blow up like an atomic bomb and make a shambles of the world around you. Then you're once again that madonna-like perfection, as unemotional as a smooth marble statue.'

'What would you have me do?' she asked calmly, sipping her coffee. 'Go into hysterics every fifteen minutes? No, I only get upset at the things I consider important, not much in this world is important, I fear.'

'Such cynicism.' He sat beside her and poured himself a cup too. 'I wish I'd thought to tell you to wake me up. I hadn't intended to fall asleep in the first place—too many things to do today.' He shot her a quick, assessing look. 'Do you want to talk?'

'No.' She shook her head. It wouldn't do any good. She was convinced of that, for they had hashed things out long ago, and she knew that when Damien had an idea in his head, no amount of argument would shift him from his decided course. If he was determined to marry the mouse, then he would do it, come hell or high water. No, the best thing to do would be to make up her mind what she was going to do and stick to that course, no matter what happened or how deep the pain was.

'All right. We won't for now, but I really think that we have some things we need to get clear between us sooner or later. Perhaps if I have time we can talk tomorrow.' He studied her frowningly for a moment as if something about her was puzzling him.

She merely smiled an acknowledgment to his suggestion without making an actual positive response. If she let him think that, it might make everything easier later on.

She came and perched on the bed to watch him finish dressing, and they spoke of light matters together, mundane, commonplace, everyday things. He asked her if she wanted help cleaning up the mess in the living room and she politely replied in the negative, saying that she would have someone come in to clean up. She asked him if he would be working late on business that evening and he answered with a yes and a sigh. The weather was mentioned, he took his time completing his toilet, and once came over to sit beside her on the bed and play with her long fingers.

She soon felt like screaming, but Damien was finally walking to the door and pausing to look down at her, a gentle, quizzical light in his eyes and a slight quirk on his lips. One hand came to cup her cheek and then his lips were coming down for a tender, lingering kiss. Then he said huskily, 'I like it when you get angry. We always make up so satisfactorily. Don't change, Jessie. You're so special just the way you are.'

He pulled the door closed behind, and she stared unseeingly at the expanse of white. What was so special about the way she was? She didn't think she was so very special. She was all tied up in knots inside, confused, hurting, and she didn't know what to do. What was so terrific about that? She was convinced that Damien was seeing the plastic, public image that she projected and not her real self. The packaging looked nice, but it wasn't real. And that was why she couldn't stand to continue seeing him. It didn't seem to mean anything when he didn't really and truly care. She felt so barren.

Rousing herself, she went over to the phone and was soon speaking to the kindly lady who did the housework and fixed meals for her. 'Hello, Mrs Marrazotto, could you perhaps come over sometime this afternoon and do a bit of picking up? I've had a slight problem in the living room and a few things were broken ... no, everything is fine, there was just an accident. I'll have the worst of it picked up, but the vacuum cleaner needs to be run over the carpet and I need to go out later. Thanks very much, see you later.'

She hesitated and felt guilty for the way she was handling things, and then, with an impatient shrug, she called the management of the apartment building. A pleasant-sounding female voice answered, and Jessica said, 'I've had a bit of an accident and have broken the glass doors up here. . . .' and she gave her apartment number and name. 'I'm more than willing to pay for the damages and labour needed to have new glass installed, if you could round up someone from maintenance for me? Oh, wonderful. And there's one more thing.' She hesitated and then took the plunge. 'I want my locks changed right away—I don't care how much it costs, as long as you have someone up by this evening to take care of it. All right. Thank you very much.'

As she replaced the receiver, she suddenly felt very tired. What was she going to do without Damien? He sometimes felt as if he were her second half, her alter ego, her completion. She felt as if a vital organ was being ripped out of her and the pain of amputation was so severe, it was nearly crippling.

Maybe she could take a nap later on in the day. She wanted quite badly to go to sleep.

CHAPTER FOUR

JESSICA paused at the front door of the Coefield residence, her hands shaking and her mouth dry. A myriad of conflicting thoughts assailed her, but in spite of them all, she raised her hand—albeit reluctantly— and rang the doorbell, though she knew that she should turn and run in the other direction as fast as she could.

The wait was short. She had just enough time to turn and admire the sunny Sunday morning, quite unlike that rainy dreariness of two days ago. The front door swung open quickly, and she turned to be confronted with the sight of Mary, dressed in drab, faded jeans and a badly fitting blouse, her mousy brown hair in wisps around her face. But in spite of her awful appearance, her face lit up with an innocent pleasure at seeing Jessica's slim, immaculate form.

'Miss King!' she exclaimed shyly, backing up immediately and beckoning for Jessica to enter. 'This is quite a surprise! Can I—er, help you with anything? Did you want to see my mother? I'm sorry to say that she's not here at the moment.'

'Oh, I didn't necessarily come to see just your mother,' Jessica replied, feeling oddly relieved that Mrs Coefield was not at home. She would rather face Mary's uncomplicated friendliness than Mrs Coefield's veiled hostility any time. 'I just thought that I'd come over for a quick visit. If it's a bad time, then I can leave. I'm afraid that I tend to do things like this on impulse.' A stupid one, she added silently.

'Oh! Oh, no, don't leave!' Mary assured her eagerly,

almost falling over her feet in her haste to back up to a door on her right. 'Please come and have a seat. Would you, um, like some coffee, or something else? Tea?'

'Coffee would be wonderful, thank you,' Jessica politely replied, and she watched with some amusement as Mary hurried out of the room to inform the cook of her visitor. The younger girl was back some minutes later, and she seemed to be all thumbs and feet as she perched herself awkwardly in a chair near Jessica's. They talked lightly together while waiting for the coffee, each busily summing up the other. Jessica saw the covert glances at her perfectly tailored trouser suit and matching suede shoes. She had to smile at the wide-eyed look Mary shot at her gleaming chignon, which gave the observer an excellent view of her high cheekbones and marvellous, strangely tinted eyes.

She found that her first reluctant impression of the younger girl still held: Mary was an unsophisticated, vulnerable, likeable person. After a time, when they had become more at ease with each other, Mary said wistfully, 'You look lovely today, Miss King. But then I've always thought you were the most beautiful woman I've ever seen. I wish I were as pretty as you.'

'Why, thank you,' Jessica replied, indifferently enough. 'But please call me Jessica. Miss King makes me feel like a schoolteacher! You know, Mary, beauty is only skin deep. It's what is inside that matters.'

Mary fumbled with the corner of her collar with an unhappy expression and Jessica wondered why they had suddenly got so deep. This was only supposed to be a light social call. The other girl said suddenly, 'Oh, I know that's true, but sometimes it doesn't help! It's very easy for you to say, too, since you're so beautiful already. I'm just an ugly duckling.

Her head darted around and she took in the strangely

lost expression on Mary's little face. It was like the expression on a stray puppy or kitten, appealing because of its very vulnerability, and something prompted her to say coolly, 'I don't believe in ugliness, Mary. I just don't believe that ugliness is necessary or even real, except maybe where evil is concerned. Beauty is an illusion, and so is ugliness. Nobody is ugly, I don't care how old or wrinkled or overweight they may be. It's just that some people may have to work harder at conforming to what society tells us is "beauty". You— yes, even you, so don't look at me that way—you could be quite lovely if you only set your mind to it and decided to be beautiful! And it's something that no amount of cosmetics or beautiful clothes will give to you. You've got to believe that you are beautiful.'

Mary listened intently, her face indicating that she found Jessica's words vitally important. 'But how?' she asked forlornly. 'I don't know how to go about being beautiful.'

Jessica regarded her for a moment and asked herself silently again, what am I doing here? Why am I sitting here? The answer eluded herself for the time being, and she sighed. 'Why is it so important?'

Mary's eyes fell. She flushed, an uneven colour and unattractive, with her spotted complexion. 'I—it's just—do you remember Damien Kent from the party Friday night?' It was an outburst, too loudly spoken, and it made Jessica jump.

The pain that hit her was intense and brief, like a knife stab in the stomach that was then miraculously healed. 'Yes,' she managed to get out calmly, 'I do.'

'I—he's so handsome and smart, and he asked me out, *me*, of all people!' Her voice was small, miserable, as if she wanted to crawl under a rock and hide, and Jessica listened to that bewildered outcry, sympathising more than Mary could know. 'And I know why, too. It's not because of me, but because of Daddy's business. He would have never looked at me otherwise. Nobody ever does.'

Jessica knew this to be true, but the quality of self-truth in one so utterly crushed by it, made her wince as if she had seen an open wound. 'Did he tell you that?' she asked, meaning to speak gently but secretly shocked at the harshness in her own voice.

Mary shook her head sadly, eyes averted. The coffee had been brought in some time ago, and they both sipped absently from their cups. Pastries had been served also and Mary was steadily nibbling through several, but Jessica politely refused. 'But why else would he ask me out?' she asked in a small voice. 'I know that he's interested in Daddy's business, and I know that he would have never taken me out otherwise. He could see anyone he wants—even you.' The pain at this artless statement was much worse than the first and Jessica knew that something odd had showed on her face. She was relieved to see that Mary was too wrapped up in her own miseries to notice. 'I wish I were beautiful. I wish somebody would ask me out for myself, not for Daddy's money.'

'How old are you, Mary?' She felt a rush of maternal feeling for this young girl, and she shouldn't be feeling it. The situation was potentially too dangerous.

'Eighteen.' The reply was dull. 'And I've never even been on a date before Friday, if you can call that a date.' Eighteen. And Damien was thirty-eight, old enough in years and experience to be this child's father. Jessica felt very old beside Mary's extreme youth and naiveté. And yet this child had enough sense to see the world with a cruel perception. She wondered what

Damien would say if he were to find out that Mary was under no illusions about him. Jessica rather suspected that he would be relieved. Then he wouldn't have to explain his position to her when he proposed. She knew that he would be as truthful to Mary as he was with herself, or for that matter any woman. Lying was not a part of his philosophy.

She couldn't understand her impulse, when she later thought everything through, and she didn't search herself too hard. Perhaps it was that sad, sad look in the other girl's eyes that prompted her. Whatever the reason, she was suddenly speaking, and she couldn't take back the words once they were uttered, and she didn't really think she wanted to.

'Mary,' she said. The girl looked up inquiringly, and the droop to her small mouth impelled Jessica to say, 'Would you realy like to be beautiful? Do you want it enough to work at it honestly, without just giving up and quitting whenever you felt like it?'

Something sparked in those brown eyes and Mary replied swiftly, 'Oh, yes! Mother's been trying to get me to go to exercise classes, but I've been too embarrassed to go all by myself. But I'd give just about anything to be attractive.'

'Well, darling,' Jessica drawled, sitting back and leisurely crossing one elegant leg over the other. 'Then we'll just have to take the little duck and make her into a swan, won't we?'

Mary's head jerked, her eyes widened, and the eager hope on her face made Jessica at once amused and yet saddened. The girl was so pathetic. Really, someone should have taken her in hand long ago. 'Are—are you saying what I think you're saying?' she asked, uncertainly.

'That rather depends on what you think I'm saying,'

Jessica returned serenely, calm now that she had committed herself.

Mary flushed again. 'I—I guess I thought you said that you would help me become more—more attractive.'

'Don't look so embarrassed, you silly goose. That's exactly what I said. You've got to promise me something,' Jessica warned, shaking a stern finger at Mary, making her laugh. 'You promise me right here and now that you will do just as I say, and you won't cheat on your diet, or give up. Otherwise, it won't work and I won't waste my time.'

'I'm going on a diet?'

'You'd better believe it, honey. And you're starting it right now, so put down that horrible Danish pastry. Now I want to hear a promise . . . good. Tell me what you usually eat in a day.' She listened to Mary's rambling and carefree recital with horror. No wonder the girl had a problem with her complexion! 'Well! I can see that we have our work cut out for us!' she exclaimed. 'Can we talk with your cook? I think we had better plan out your meals before I go.'

Mary dutifully called in the cook, a plump, pleasant woman who listened respectfully to Jessica's orders. 'First of all,' she said briskly, 'I want you to go on a twenty-four hour fast. Are you doing anything strenuous tomorrow? That's all right, then. Take things easy and drink only water, as much as you like. We're going to clean out your system. After the fast, you are going on such a strict diet, you won't be able to sneeze without permission. Worried?'

Becoming wildly excited now, in spite of Jessica's determinedly matter-of-fact voice, Mary shook her head enthusiastically.

'Good, though you really should be. Diets are hard

work until you refuse the fattening things in restaurants by force of habit. And once you start a diet, you usually are on it for life. Now, I want you to understand that this is only the first step. You can diet all you want and you will still gain back all of the weight you lose if you break the diet without exercising. Your body has what is called a "set point" and the only way that you can lower your individual set point is by exercise. And when you lower your set point, your body then says that it's okay to keep that extra weight off, because you are using your intake of food more efficiently by raising your metabolism rate. But we won't start the exercise until we get you used to eating healthily. . . .' Jessica then turned to the cook and talked with her for some time, working out a diet for Mary that contained only certain foods. She smiled at the younger girl after a while and said, 'Well, that's that. Your cook can figure out a thoroughly nutritious meal plan from the four food groups, and I'll leave you my number so that you can call me in two weeks.'

Mary blinked. 'Is that it?' she asked in confusion. 'You aren't going to show me any make-up techniques, or take me shopping?' She sounded so disappointed that Jessica had to laugh.

'Darling, I have to have something to work from before we start all that. First we must clear up your complexion and slim down your figure. This is the ground work; you won't even get anywhere near the other things if you don't start learning healthy habits. In two weeks we're going to start that exercise programme—yes, I'll go with you at first—and then we'll perhaps think of the rest. And now,' she smiled and stood gracefully, 'I've overstayed my welcome. Call me when you begin to lose weight, love, and don't starve yourself, or become a fanatic about all this. After all, healthiness is what it's all about, and fanaticism is not healthy. But don't snack! See you later.'

On the way back to her apartment Jessica had time to sit back and wonder at her impulsive offer. She was getting herself into something deeper than she had first expected. She had seen the beginnings of hero worship in Mary's star-bright eyes, and she didn't want to have adolescent adoration on her hands, on top of everything else. Mary appeared to think that Jessica was going to wave a magic wand over her and transform her into that graceful swan, but it didn't work that way. She had to do the work herself. Jessica was just going to nudge her in the right direction now and then. And, she thought whimsically, take her to someone who would sell her the right type of clothes for her figure.

How Mary handled her other problem was strictly between herself and Damien. She was only going to help a little in the self-esteem department. She admitted to herself quite candidly, in the privacy of her car, that she hoped if Mary began to feel and look more attractive, she might begin to date boys more her own age and eventually forget about Damien. Hopefully she would lean in that direction, since she was under no illusions about him, but there was the danger that with a more attractive appearance she might be able to interest him in herself and not just her father's business. Who knows? Jessica shrugged philosophically and then winced. Damien just may fall in love with her. It would be, she thought cynically, very convenient.

It didn't really matter to her any more, one way or another. And that was the biggest lie in history, she acknowledged ruefully, because it would always matter to her. Back at her apartment she collapsed as if she had just run a marathon race. She suspected, though, that the marathon was just beginning. Life would certainly be a struggle for a while. She hoped that Damien wouldn't find out what she was up to.

A quick, cool shower helped to refresh her, and she was sitting in front of the television with a lemon and soda, thinking about her next modelling assignment, when the phone rang. She jumped a mile high at the sound, more from apprehension than from being startled. She knew just who it would be, and when she picked up the receiver and spoke into it, she found she wasn't wrong.

'Hello, Damien.' Her voice was calm, even flat, and certainly not indicative of the kind of tension that was gripping her in the stomach and churning up the liquid she had already drunk.

'Hello, darling,' he replied huskily. 'I tried to call earlier but you were out. Did you have a nice day?'

'Fair. I just—shopped. And you?'

'About the same. I've been going over reports. Shall I be over in about an hour, or would you like a little more time?'

'Damien, I don't think you'd better come over,' she said hesitantly, the words having a tendency to stick in her throat. This was going to be harder than she had first supposed.

'Would later be better then?'

From his unconcerned attitude she realised that he hadn't fully understood what she was trying to say, and she swallowed. It wasn't surprising, in view of how she had always welcomed him before. It would be a shock, even though she knew that he didn't love her, for he had to care to some extent to stay with her for three years. Oh God, how could she give it up?

'No, Damien,' she heard herself say gently, and she wanted to take it back so badly that tears started up in her eyes, but all she did was to listen to the utter silence at the other end.

'What do you mean?' he asked quietly, at last, and she nearly groaned aloud. He would make her say it, plainly and succintly. That was Damien.

'I don't think we should see each other any more.' I love you. 'This is no longer the type of relationship I want to have.' I want you. 'I don't want to see you again, Damien, I'm sorry.' And as the words dropped out of her mouth, she said to herself silently, liar.

Quiet. And then, 'What has brought this on?' His voice sounded queer, as if he had been hit in the abdomen, and she knew that he was feeling something akin to the pain that she had been feeling for the past few days. She was nearly overwhelmed with her sympathy for him and a love so strong that it began to undermine her determination.

'I don't want to talk about it right now, if you don't mind,' she said politely. 'Several things have been bothering me lately, and let's just leave it at that.' Like, I'm tearing up inside with jealousy and pain, and it makes me so full of unhappiness and anger that I can't stand it. Like, I'm going to fall apart if we keep going the way we were going.

'Like hell, we'll leave it at that!' he rasped out, furiously. 'You can't do this, just like that, on the telephone, you cold-blooded——' He bit off what he was about to say. When he spoke next, he was so calm and unemotional, it had her puzzled and worried. 'Justin. You are going to marry him.'

What was he thinking now? she asked silently. What was he feeling? 'No, I'm not marrying Justin and, contrary to popular belief, I am not sleeping with him. It has nothing to do with him, it's strictly between you and me.' And a third, innocent, unsuspecting party. 'Things just haven't been right.'

'You seemed to derive a great deal of satisfaction out of "things" the other day,' he drawled sarcastically, and she winced from the bite of it. 'Why the sudden change of heart, darling? Did you find someone richer?'

She sucked in her breath, audibly, harshly, and found herself shaking so violently from the hurt and the anger at such an obviously false implication that she had been after his money, that she could hardly put the phone receiver back on the hook. And as she settled it gently back into place, she could still hear his voice calling urgently to her. A few tears fell to splash on her tightly clenched hands, and she wiped them away angrily, pressing her lips together as hard as she could. She would not cry, she would not cry, she would not. She could not. Control it, control it, Jessica, she told herself, and another tear fell. Why did he have to tear her up so?

The phone shrilled, the sound angry and loud to her. Her head jerked to it involuntarily and she didn't want to answer, didn't want to talk to him, didn't want to think or hurt ... and she found herself holding the phone receiver in one white-knuckled hand. She slowly raised it to her ear and listened.

'—don't hang up, Jessica! Are you there?' he asked abruptly, and she hesitated before answering.

'Yes.' A bare thread of a sound.

'I'm sorry. It was a foul and inaccurate thing to say to you,' he continued, his liquid voice not as smooth as usual.

'Yes.'

'Look, Jessica, surely you can see that this is not the way to settle things! I'm coming over right now and we'll talk this out properly,' he stated arrogantly. His voice was cool and decisive, but she could still feel the thread of anger running through it and she felt suddenly cold.

'You won't be able to get in. I've changed my locks,' she said clearly, and began to quake.

Silence, and then an explosion from the other end. 'I'm coming up,' he said grimly, 'and you're going to open that door and talk to me, damn it! This is no way to end a relationship! Be your age, for God's sake! Or had you actually contemplated a "dear John" letter as an alternative?'

The hateful sneer made her break down and before she could catch herself, a tiny sob shuddered through her chest, and she clapped a hand to her mouth, horrified. Everything inside her seemed to be crumbling, like a house made out of playing cards that begins to fall. 'No, Damien,' she whispered. 'I wanted to tell you in person, but was afraid that you would try to make me change my mind and tear me apart inside, like you are now and that's why I can't see you anymore, darling, I—it's just too——'

'Just what do you think you're doing to me?' he asked raggedly. 'I've never known you to be this way. What's got into you, for God's sake? Why won't you *talk to me*?'

'No strings, Damien!' she moaned, feeling trapped by the urgency in his voice. Why was he putting her through all this? Was his pride that injured by her rejection? She could see that: Damien was great at loving and then leaving. The woman probably never got the chance. 'That's what you made me promise to you a long time ago! No strings. Well, I need to walk away right now, because I'm finding there isn't anything to really make me want to stay. I—don't come. It won't do any good. I daren't let you in. Goodbye, Damien. I hope you're happy.'

She hung up on him for the second time and went into her bedroom. There, unable to hold in her desolation and devastation, she cried her eyes out. The phone rang at different intervals, long and insistent, until she finally unplugged it. It was a long and lonely night.

Finding herself feeling a sort of desperation now that she had committed herself finally, she told the secretary at the modelling agency that she was no longer accepting calls from Mr Kent. And she lived like a zombie for the next several days, staggering to work and falling in a heap at home in the evenings. She lost weight she couldn't afford to lose, circles appeared under her eyes, and the sparkle in them died away. They looked a strange, dull yellow, as if the unique golden colour had come from the fire in her spirit rather than the actual shade in the iris, and they contained a strangely brittle glassiness, like marbles.

Finally her photographer, Jeff, told her in disgust that she had better have a vacation before she lost all of her looks. She chuckled dryly at first and then looked at him oddly. The idea was a good one. Perhaps she needed to get out of town for a while, put a little distance between herself and the memory of Damien, and gain a little perspective.

That was just about the time that Mary called her.

She listened patiently to Mary's enthusiastic speech, reflecting mildly at how the dieting and weight loss seemed to have given her a new vivacity. She had totally forgotten about her promise to the other girl and felt a sinking heart at the thought of seeing her again. None of this showed in her voice, though, as she calmly congratulated Mary on her hard work and suggested various times when she would be free to go exercising. They worked out a few mutually satisfying times and then Jessica promised that she would check out the rates of her favourite health spa.

She did so faithfully, calling Mary back, and arranged to meet her at the spa the very next day. She arrived at the designated time, reluctantly, and was genuinely amazed at the girl that bounced down the front sidewalk to greet her. 'Mary! Good heavens, losing just a few pounds did wonders for you! I am very, very impressed!' she exclaimed with a frank astonishment. The weight loss was very apparent and her complexion had cleared dramatically with her healthier diet.

Mary's little face beamed. 'I was so hoping you'd notice! Doesn't it look fabulous? Only, none of my clothes fit anymore.' She turned on her heel for Jessica and threw her arms around herself excitedly.

Jessica had to smile at that, a genuine smile, and her first in days. 'And your clothes are going to look even more strange in a few weeks when your muscles start to tone up and give you an even different shape. You're going to learn everything from posture to push ups, my girl! Come on, or we'll be late.'

And so they exercised regularly, four times a week together for a few weeks. Damien had not tried to contact Jessica in that time, and she didn't know whether to be happy about that or sad. She only knew that she was lonelier now than she had ever been before. She only knew that she yearned for Damien's hard arms around her and his sweet, gentle smile more than she had ever before, and nothing seemed to be bright or cheerful.

She took one look at Mary's healthy, glowing face after one exercise session and decided that it was time for the younger girl to get a treat for her hard work. True to her word, Mary had not let one pastry, chocolate, or sip of liquor past her lips, and it showed. She was definitely looking better, slimmer, more vital, and she confessed to an increase in energy.

'How would you like a reward?' Jessica asked her, a slight smile tugging at her pale, beautifully formed lips. She was wearing a minimum of make-up since they had just finished showering, and she had to admit that the exercising had been good for her too.

'Like what?' Mary asked interestedly, skipping a little from sheer exuberance. Jessica had to smile at the psychology that she privately termed the "beautifying process". Something magical happened to a woman when she went through this. Jessica thought that it must be because of the work and the time involved, together with the figure changing visibly for the better. One actually began to think and feel that she really was attractive, and that was one of the secrets to beauty, actually believing that you can be beautiful. Bone structure, eye make-up and pretty clothes were merely props.

'Like a nice big, luscious piece of chocolate cake with ice cream?' she suggested. Mary looked startled.

'Are you actually going to have something fattening?' the younger girl asked incredulously. 'I don't think I've ever seen you eat anything rich.' Jessica shook her head with a sleepy look that hid watching eyes.

'But you could have something if you wanted,' she replied. 'After all, you've worked hard. You deserve a treat.'

'Oh, no you don't! You aren't getting me off my diet just when I've started to do so well!' Mary said flatly. Her eyes popped out when Jessica burst into a pleased laughter.

'My dear,' she drawled, 'I'm quite proud of you, really! You've now graduated to the third step. Feel like going shopping and getting a few make-up lessons and a hair cut?'

'Really?' Mary sounded so wonderfully pleased, as if Jessica was a surrogate Santa Claus come to this earth specifically for her very own Christmas. 'Is it already time for that? I'd love it! When do we do it?'

'I have an appointment for you with an old friend of mine in about a half an hour. I checked with your mother to make sure you were free. Is that all right?'

'Oh, boy, it certainly is!' And so the afternoon was spent, with Jessica whirling Mary into different shops for a while to emerge later with both of their arms laden with packages. Jessica watched while her friend Clarisse worked expertly on Mary's little face, and after two hours they left with Mary transformed into a vivacious, attractive girl clutching a small bag which held a fortune in cosmetics. Then Jessica took her to her own hairdresser and after an expert cut and a henna treatment to bring out the red highlights in her mousy brown hair, Mary looked like a totally different person.

Jessica had obtained Mrs Coefield's unreserved approval for the shopping spree. Mrs Coefield had barely recognised her own daughter after going to a few exercise sessions, and her initial hostility had long since evaporated to a gratified and pleased warmth towards Jessica. With an unlimited budget Jessica now took Mary around to the boutiques and various shops that she frequented herself, picking out a lavish wardrobe for her, watching the younger girl's eyes grow round with horror and delight at the amount of money spent. She incidentally spent quite a lot on herself, too, as certain outfits caught her eye. She picked out clothes that corrected Mary's shorter legs and waist, with slightly padded, severely tailored shoulders, to hide her sloping shoulders. No amount of posture practice had enabled Mary to overcome that physical defect. She stuck to plainer styles for Mary, not wanting to overwhelm her with too many frills and flounces, and still being rather conventional, sensing that the younger girl did not have the flair or the desire to carry off the more dramatic outfits as she did.

Mary gave her an impulsive hug when she parked her car in front of the Coefield residence, the back seat laden down with all sorts of boxes and bags bearing expensive designer names. After the first surprised moment, Jessica hugged her back. She had become very fond of Mary and really did wish her the best. And although it hurt her very much to admit it, she hoped that if Damien and Mary were to be married then she wanted everything to work out between the two.

She went in for a brief drink and to listen with a tolerant amusement as Mary bubbled over with excitement, telling her mother all about the various shops and what they had bought, what they had nearly bought, and what they would never have bought. The other two women could hardly get a word in edgewise in the unbroken stream of patter. Her speech was littered with, 'Jessica says this', or 'Jessica thinks that', and Mrs Coefield shared a long understanding look with Jessica, sending her a warm, grateful smile. She opted, instead of the cocktail proffered, for her usual lemon and soda, and Mary followed her lead, confessing that she was finally beginning to like the taste of lemon in her drink and she would probably never drink anything else. Jessica finally escaped after many invitations to supper and admonitions to call and visit. She drove away thoughtfully, her golden eyes regretful. She didn't really expect to see Mary or the rest of the Coefields again, and it was a pity since she had begun to like them all very much.

She pulled into her parking space, in an underground garage especially for the tenants in her apartment building, and she got out of her car automatically, her mind busy and her air distracted. She reached into the back of the car to get her various purchases and, loaded down, turned to make her way to the elevator.

'Can I help you with anything?' The deep, smooth, attractive masculine voice was so familiar, and had been familiar for three years. She recognised that voice immediately and her heart started to thump after one shocked moment, her eyes glazing and ears roaring. She did not even have to turn around to know who stood behind her, and so when she did move it was to turn leisurely, in an effort to hide her shock.

'Damien. What are you doing here?' she asked quietly. Her eyes were expressively leaping into life again with the fierce pleasure and intense pain of seeing him, actually, physically seeing him after close to five weeks. A lifetime in just five weeks.

He looked good, too good. His black hair shone in a way she seemed to have nearly forgotten and his eyes were so alive, so dark and expressively vivid. His lean cheeks were slightly more hollow under the cheekbones, making his jaw more prominent. One of his eyebrows was cocked at her and that, too, was so familiar that, with heart aching and eyes stinging, she turned away from him to walk determinedly towards the elevator doors.

'Don't I even get an, "It's good to see you again, how're you doing" greeting?' he asked her quizzically, falling into step beside her.

'Go away.' She increased her pace, hopelessly, and sure enough, he smoothly increased his pace right along with her.

'Funny. I could have sworn that just now you were

happy to see me. However, looks can be deceiving, I know. Come now, Jessica, don't you know me well enough to realise that when I have my heart set on something, I usually attain it? You knew that I was determined to talk to you—surely you didn't delude yourself into thinking that your puny efforts to keep me away would really work, did you?' He might have been talking about the new paint job on the basement concrete walls, so little expression was in his voice, and yet he had her trembling in reaction, a violent, telltale response.

Had that really been what she had expected? Had she really expected him to come after her and demand a confrontation? She was profoundly shocked, not only at Damien's sudden appearance but at the way she had successfully deluded herself. She hadn't really wanted to break things off with him. She had expected him to be more persistent, to chase after her, to follow her and force a confrontation. That was why she had felt so let down in the last few weeks, so depressed and unsatisfied. She had decided that he really didn't care, one way or the other, because he hadn't pressed the issue.

Now he was here, looking suddenly grim and falling silent, his eyes trained on her, hawklike, perceptive. She turned her face away, to give herself time to control her expression, and she pushed the elevator button with one awkward finger, juggling her packages. She didn't know how to treat this potentially explosive man and touchy situation. She felt so inadequate for this confrontation. She kept her face turned away, and was silent also.

The doors opened and she stepped quickly in, not looking at Damien, and she said, 'It's no use. I'm not inviting you in, so you might as well go now.'

He didn't bother to reply and just calmly stepped into the elevator, the implacable stern look on his strongly featured face coupled with the dark beginnings of a smouldering flame in his eyes making her knees shake.

'I would have been here sooner, except that I've been to Europe on business,' he said finally, conversationally, the sound of his voice in the small confines of the cubicle making her jump.

'Everything go all right?' she asked lightly. She had to moisten her lips and with a quick sideways glance found him watching the movement of her tongue intently, with a strange hunger, and this frightened her so that she cried out suddenly, 'Why don't you go away and leave me alone?'

A muscle leapt in his jaw and his eyes shuttered over, masking that unguarded look, and he snapped grimly, 'Because I'm not satisfied with the inadequate conversation we had a few weeks ago, and I want some explanations, Jessica. I've begun to think that you haven't been nearly as open with me as I'd originally thought, and it's not a pleasant feeling.'

'There's nothing to say,' she said coldly, marching out of the elevator as the doors opened and trying to ignore Damien as he relentlessly followed. 'I don't want to see you any more. Period. End of explanation, end of story, have a nice life and get out of my way, will you?'

'Why have you been seeing Mary Coefield?' That quiet voice was worse than anything Justin, in all of his years as a lawyer, had produced. She hated it; she hated him; she began to feel angry at this post mortem on their relationship and, secretly, had to admit that part of the anger she was feeling was stemming from feeling frightened and threatened. He was intent on undermining all of her good intentions and digging into feelings that she was trying her best to suppress. Just seeing him again was making her shake from a terrible weakness. What would she do if he tried to make love to her, wrap those warm arms around her, press his lips on hers and caress her body with those wonderful hands? She felt a wave of longing and love so strong that it made her dizzy, and with the dizziness came a wave of pure rage. She felt so out of control with him, so helpless and vulnerable. She had to prevent that, to keep from succumbing to her feelings and yearnings at all cost.

She suddenly sagged just outside her apartment, as if from resignation, and then handed all of her packages to Damien. 'Would you, please?' she asked absently. His hands came out automatically for them and, brain working furiously, she fumbled in her purse for her door key and fitted it into the lock casually and slowly, limbs shaking. She'd only have a split second, the element of surprise, and she'd have to grasp at the chance boldly, otherwise all would be lost. 'I guess I just thought she would be happier with a better self-image, poor thing. . . .' As the lock came free and she turned the handle, she pushed the door open as if to enter it normally and then leaped inside to slam the door shut again hard, hands snaking to the bolt and chain on the inside of the door, hearing Damien drop the packages immediately to leap at the door also and lean against it furiously. His hard body slammed against the firm oak and she heard swearing. He had been just that one split second too late. She'd got the bolt home in time.

'Damn you, damn you, *damn* you!' he shouted, and brought his heavy fist down on the door, and sturdy though it was, it shuddered with the impact. 'Jessica, so help me, if you don't open this door, when I finally get a hold of you, I swear I'm going to wring your obstinate neck!' It was a full-throated roar of rage and she automatically stepped back as if that would give her more protection.

'No, I can't!' she shouted back. 'I just can't see you, Damien! Don't you know how you tear me up inside? Will you just go away? I don't want this—just leave my packages by the door and get out of here, will you?'

'By God, I won't!' he swore, pounding the door in frustration. She thought that she could actually see it vibrate, and began to wonder if it would hold. The door had seemed so solid in the past, but it didn't seem half as dependable now. 'If I have to, I'll break this door down! Do you hear me? Now open up, Jessica, before I get so furious I do something I might regret!'

'No! Go away!' She backed away even further, her sophistication falling away like a discarded cloak and in its place leaving a frightened, uncertain girl.

She heard him swearing steadily, viciously, on the other side of the door and then there was a sudden brief silence that had her wondering. Her puzzlement didn't last for long, though, for seconds later there was an almighty crash as something solid and powerful hit her oaken front door. She actually did see it shudder this time. Silence again, and then another, louder, harder crash, and the walls shook. She had time to think that perhaps she really should go and open up the door before he tore up the apartment building, and then a third crash splintered the door's lock and Damien surged into the living room like a powerful tidal wave or a marauding animal. He certainly looked animalistic, bestial, with hair falling on his brow and wide chest heaving, and his lips drawn back to show white, gritted teeth. He pulled to a stop, face grim, and just looked at her.

Jessica swallowed once, and then quietly backed away from him until she was across the room, feeling a fear that she had never expected to associate with the one she loved.

CHAPTER FIVE

SOMETHING flitted across Damien's face at her retreat, some quick, fleeting expression. It had looked like pain, but she couldn't be sure. She was too busy trying to decide what he would do next to really pay attention to his changing expressions. She was too busy trying to overcome her own fears. Deciding that, in Justin's words, offence was a good defence, she put her hands to her hips and demanded, 'Now you've done it, and all I've got to say is that you'd better buy me another door, Damien Kent!'

'Don't you ever, ever lock that door against me again,' he commanded furiously, and she nodded, all of her bravado slipping away like trickling water. He would only break it down again, like he had this one, and she didn't really want to have broken doors all over the place. She could not force Damien out of her apartment and out of her life and she was beginning to realise that. She could only persuade him that it was best for him to leave. He looked at her frowningly, as if at a loss, and then he asked her, 'Why did you do it? You know how that infuriates me.'

She just looked at him. 'I don't know. I guess I didn't particularly care whether you got angry or not. I just didn't want you to come inside.'

Her candid reply had made him angry again, she could tell. His lips tightened and his eyes darkened. He looked fed up and then he expelled a short, gusty breath and relaxed. 'Fair enough. I ask for the truth so I can't complain when I get it. I just don't understand you any more, Jess. What happened? Why did you change towards me so suddenly, from one day to the next? You must realise that you can't cut off a relationship that has lasted for three years without some kind of explanation. Dammit, will you talk to me?'

She smiled, an angry, helpless, mirthless smile and shook her head. 'I don't know what to say to you. What do you want to hear from me? That I've found a new lover, or that I just got tired of you? Do you want me to wrap everything up in a nice, neat little package so that you can file everything away in old records? What difference does it make what my motives are for breaking up our relationship? And why should I feel obligated to explain anything in a no-strings agreement? I wanted out, so I got out. And by the way, are you going to buy me a new door?'

His head jerked and his eyes narrowed warningly on her. 'Forget the door for a minute, will you? Look, the reason why I want to know what the hell is going on is because I want to know if it's me, something I should change about myself. Did I do something? What did you expect from me?'

Unaccountably, surprised by the strange note of pleading in his voice, Jessica sat down suddenly and stared up at him with huge questioning eyes. He stood with both hands resting on his slim hips, his shoulders thrown back in a naturally straight posture, legs planted well apart. He would have looked as if he were an ancient landowner surveying all he owned, except for that expression on his face. He wore a puzzled frown and not only looked uncertain but very frustrated also.

How could she explain to him without giving away her true feelings? How could she communicate to him just what she was struggling to deal with? 'I think I need a drink,' she muttered, not looking at him as she quickly rose to go and pour herself a stiff whisky. The liquid burned her throat but warmth immediately began to seep throughout her midriff in a soothing way. 'I got this liquor cabinet in Virginia, did I tell you? It's an antique from eighteenth-century England. Lovely wood.... So you've seen Mary recently, have you? How do you think she's looking?'

He frowned again, impatiently, and then his brow cleared and he came over to lean against the couch, one foot kicked over the other as he considered her question. 'I saw her yesterday, and yes, the change in her is astounding. She's like another girl altogether. Why did you do it, Jess? That's surely going a bit too far into the realm of the fantastic, isn't it, the mistress helping the wife to be?'

Her eyes dulled; whatever she had felt when he had crashed into her apartment, it had certainly sparked up the expression in her eyes until that last statement of his. 'I'm not your mistress,' she said quietly. 'And I did it because she needed a friend, someone who liked her for what she was and was willing to help her to become what she was capable of being. Of all the people that child is surrounded with, no one seemed to be able to see how she was needing just a little support and a good push in the right direction. I did it because she was feeling miserable that you were seeing her and you weren't doing it for her sake but for her father's assets, and she needed some reassurance that she was an attractive person in her own right. I did it because I had no intention of seeing you when you got married, and I wanted you both to be as happy as possible together, if that doesn't sound terribly conceited of me.'

'I think I know what you mean,' he said slowly, his shoulders stooping ever so slightly. 'I haven't yet asked her to marry me, Jess. There's no guarantee that she would have me, That's not the real reason why you don't want to see me anymore.'

'Yes it is, darling,' she replied sadly, swirling the amber liquid in her glass and looking at the light reflected in it thoughtfully. She absently held it out to him. She always gave him the rest of whatever drink she happened to have, when she had drunk enough, and he always had finished off her meals in a restaurant when she could eat no more. He took the glass as automatically as she had offered it and tossed off the rest in one swallow. She suddenly realised the intimacy of the small exchange and smiled ruefully. In some ways they were still so close. 'You see, it's not whether you actually marry her or not that even matters to me anymore, though of course it does. I'm not making much sense, I know. It's just that it is a bit of a blow to my feminine pride to see you offer for her instead of for me, and that's why it matters. But it really doesn't matter if you actually ask her or not, it's the fact that you would even consider it while involved in a relationship with me that matters. I don't want that kind of relationship anymore, Damien. That's no good. It's—immoral, I guess.'

'You see it that way and yet you've slept with a man you haven't been married to for three years. I believe that it's called fornication, my dear,' he said dryly, standing to go and pour himself another whisky. 'You appear to have strange ideas about morality. Absolved of sin on the one hand and yet sin by intention on the other. You need to get your outlook on life a little clearer, don't you think?'

'No,' she said abruptly, her voice clear and decisive, her eyes taking on a determined expression. 'Fornication has nothing to do with it. I'd feel as immoral and as cheapened if you were married to me and had someone else as your mistress. The marriage vows don't mean a thing unless they are held sacred, and that's why I think that many marriages aren't real but are a mere legality on a slip of useless paper. That's why the sin by intention still holds. Our relationship hasn't been satisfactory—and don't look at me that way, it wasn't just you but me too—and a marriage certificate would not have made things right between us. Because you can actually contemplate asking someone else to marry you is a symptom that something is wrong, not necessarily the wrong action itself, although personally I would hold it as such. It's a symptom of the greater illness, which would be our relationship. I have to believe that, Damien, because if I thought for one minute that you and I had only a purely physical relationship, then that would make me a whore in my own eyes and I would rather not view myself as such. Therefore, I have to believe that something was lacking in our relationship and wrong at its very foundations for you to seek an alliance elsewhere. Haven't you realised yet that a "no-strings" relationship just doesn't exist? It's a contradiction in terms, because if you have a relationship, then you are going to feel ties of affection and loyalty. I had to end everything before I lost all of my self-respect. I just didn't have enough money or material assets to satisfy you, did I?'

She hadn't watched his expression as she spoke; indeed, she couldn't bring herself to look at him at all, and so she was quite unprepared for his sudden violent movement as he surged to his feet. Her eyes flew to him in alarm. Sure enough, he whirled on her, grabbed her by the shoulders so hard she thought something would break, and held her as though he would dearly love to shake her. She stared up into his eyes and found such a look of agony, of pain and frustration and helplessness, that she was profoundly shocked. 'God!' he ground out, and threw her away from him to turn and pace the room. 'Is that all you think we had? Is that how you rate our relationship, by material possessions?'

'Isn't that how you've rated it?' she returned quietly. He didn't answer, and she knew he wouldn't. He couldn't. If he said no, then the only thing to do would be to ask her to marry him, and she knew he wasn't prepared to do that. If he said yes, then by admission, he was conceding that she was right to end everything.

He turned to her and pointed a finger as if in accusation. 'You want me!' It was a statement, not a question. She didn't bother to refute it. He told the truth.

'But I don't want what we had any more,' she replied softly, 'and that's the key to every reason why I believe we should break up. It's too late, darling, because it's just no good any longer.'

He reached as if goaded, striding up to her to fold his arms around her masterfully, his head swooping down to force a kiss on her straight, stiff lips. He ground his mouth into hers, pulling her close to the whole length of his body, an insistent hand against the small of her back to hold her in place. He went on and on, changing the mood of the embrace from one of violence to one of tenderness, brushing his mouth tantalisingly over hers, touching his tongue delicately to the bruised areas, moulding the sides of her head and neck with his sensitive fingers.

She found it nearly impossible to remain un-responsive, but somehow she managed it. She let her body go limp, kept her lips closed against his, and let her arms hang loosely. He would never know how close she came to giving in and winding her arms eagerly around his neck, for she was let go as swiftly as she had been seized, and he was standing back to stare at her in astonishment and bafflement.

'You see?' she whispered, shaking inside, falling apart at the seams. 'I was right, it just isn't good anymore.'

'I could take you right now and you wouldn't be able to do anything about it,' he hissed, furiously, and yet the bafflement and the hurt remained underneath it all so that she saw from his threat a kind of vulnerability that she had never seen before. It made her gentle.

'That's true,' she agreed softly. 'And every inch of the way, you would know just how unwilling I would really be. And what kind of victory would that be, my love? Just what kind of triumph?'

He turned his head away as if he were unable to bear what he had just heard and he stood there for a long time, just staring blankly at nothing, head bowed slightly, shoulders slumped. And then he just walked away. He paused by the ruined door and said quietly, 'I'll call someone about coming over right away to repair your door, Jess. Don't forget your packages out here.' Then he was gone, out the door, out of her life, and everything was finished for good this time.

The utter desolation she felt was the worst emotion it had ever been her misfortune to experience.

Moving like the old woman she felt she was, Jessica went out into the hall to gather up her purchases uncaringly, stuffing shopping bags with expensive silk blouses under her arm randomly and kicking the last box in with one careless foot. She automatically turned to shut the door and had to smile thinly at the chaos Damien had managed to leave behind him.

That had always been the case. He had created chaos in her life from the very beginning, coming like a whirlwind and leaving when it suited him to, destroying her peace of mind and wrecking her calm and generating in her such a feeling of destructive rage for his unfeeling, thoughtless assumption that she would always be there for his exclusive pleasure. He had taken her body with a fine and careless arrogant ease and had plundered the recesses of her mind whenever he felt the urge for stimulating conversation, and the worst aspect of the whole affair was that she had let him come and go and had given him the right to treat her as if she were just a bit of chattel for his convenient use. And so part of the rage that she had so often felt had been directed at herself.

She was not the kind of woman that could put up with that sort of cavalier attitude. She was someone who needed an equal companionship, needed someone with whom she felt at ease enough to be as weak as she felt or as strong as she could be, with either the tears or the triumphs, the depths or the heights. She didn't really feel that she could show all aspects of her personality to anyone, and that she didn't have the type of friend that would appreciate the complexity of her personality. She wanted a lover who would know when to be tender and giving and know when to take what she had to offer. Her relationship with Damien had been so one-sided for so long, with her giving all of the time and him doing all of the taking, and she felt as though she had been wrung dry.

And yet she missed him, as she chatted lightly with the repairman who came and worked on her door, and the missing was like a wide gaping hole torn on the inside of her chest, bleeding internally, unnoticed by outsiders. She wanted what she knew instinctively Damien had inside him to give, wanted it intensely, despairingly, because she knew that she was not the woman to inspire him to feel that way. She was the loneliest person in the world, because she felt that she was truly alone, abandoned, adrift. And it didn't help for her to intellectually realise that she had been the one to break things off with him, not the other way around.

She didn't know if she could handle the sight of Damien with another woman, and she realised that with their similar circle of friends and acquaintances, sooner or later she would see him in public and, Damien being the virile man he was, she knew that she would not see him alone. How would she cope? How could she? And what would happen if, in the midst of a crowd of chattering people, he would lift his black head to search the room, and cock his eyebrow at her in that gentle, quizzical way he reserved just for her? And what would happen if she saw him look at another woman like that?

The thought was intolerable. She would probably go berserk with the pain.

She definitely loved him too much.

And over the course of the days, as her situation remained intolerable and she was forced to see that she needed to give herself time to gain a measure of serenity, she decided to leave town. She decided to go home. It was time to take an extended vacation, to re-evaluate her lifestyle, goals and ambitions. It was time to come to terms with the fact that she would never have a life with Damien, a hope that she had managed to keep alive for too long. She had to let go of illusions, false hopes, and try to build up something new again.

She called her father and found that he would be only too delighted to have her stay with him. Will King was retired now, and had been a widower for several years. He had found that, with time weighing heavily on his hands, he needed something to keep himself occupied, and so he ran a small bookshop, more for something to do than for any real need for the income. The business was tolerable, but his real love was to fish, which he indulged every chance he got, hiring a shop assistant in the summertime to have plenty of time to spend outdoors. Now was the time of year when he was in between the Christmas rush at the store and the summer's activities, and he sounded quite pleased that Jessica would be spending some time with him.

She felt a twinge of regret and guilt when she had finished talking with her father. He was getting older now, and was slowing down, though for a man in his seventies he was still remarkably fit. She loved him very much and suddenly realised that he would not be around for very much longer. He refused to spend much time in a big city, and with her active lifestyle, she had rarely had the time to make any trips to Vermont to see him. She would have to change that, would have to spend more time with him while she still had the chance. This would be a good time to get to know him all over again, and hopefully get to know herself in the process.

After letting Justin know where she would be staying and also after getting everything wrapped up at work, Jessica prepared for the trip by packing casual clothes and tidying up her apartment. It took some time and effort to arrange everything, for the modelling agency was not too happy at her unexpected leave, but as she had been looking particularly haggard lately and was long overdue for a good vacation anyway, they could do nothing but grumble.

She looked around at the apartment one last time as she was about to lock the door finally and carry down her last suitcase, and she couldn't feel any regret at leaving. The apartment was sterile and lifeless without Damien. She realised, as she looked around with newly assessing eyes, that she had decorated the place to look like a hotel, impersonal, accommodating most tastes, and it suddenly occurred to her that she had not really lived here at all but merely stayed awhile in one place. It was as if she had subconsciously known that she would be staying only a short time in this place, for she had moved into this apartment when she had started her relationship with Damien. It would be appropriate if she left the apartment now that they had broken up.

The last suitcase was stored in the back seat of her car and the seat buckle fastened around her thin waist. She briefly considered the shoulder belt but rejected the idea of putting it on. She hated to be so confined on long trips, no matter how comfortable the strap was, and she was a good driver. Dismissing it from her mind almost immediately, she started the car, reversed, and was soon coming out of the parking garage.

A great deal of time was spent just getting out of New York City, and she breathed a sigh of relief as she pulled on to a ramp that put her on an interstate highway. Once on the highway she made much better time, soon rolling down her window and letting the cool crisp air sweep through the interior of the car, for it was unseasonably warm and balmy. The sun shone very brightly and all of the trees had begun to take on the appearance of newness as tiny leaves sprouted into a fresh bright green. She felt the muscles in her back and shoulders begin to loosen and a smile tilted the corners of her lips.

She knew that afternoon that everything would be all right. She didn't try to figure out how or why she knew and she didn't worry about her future without Damien. The essence of happiness was, after all, living for the moment and taking joy from life no matter what the circumstances.

As she thought of this, in a flash of intuition Jessica realised that Damien was not a happy man. She had told Justin once that he was a troubled man, and she hadn't known then how comprehensive those words really were. Damien, for all of his envied position in the business world and for all of his material wealth, was truly unhappy. She hoped that he would come to grips with whatever it was that haunted him. She wished him the very best, no matter what happened.

Jessica had to be truthful and admit that she had been afraid to let go, to give up what small claim she had had on Damien. She had based her whole life's happiness on him and that was part of the reason why their relationship had failed. A lot of the fault had been hers. You had to give and take happiness in a relationship, just like you had to give and take love and support and caring. It was too much pressure on one individual, to be the focus of so much need. The time and the solace that she had given to him throughout those long lonely nights had not been entirely real, and she felt very sad about that. It was like saying, 'I love you' just to hear a response. It wasn't a true gift, because she had been expecting, hoping, demanding something back. There had been a lot more wrong in their relationship than she had first supposed.

Still there had been a great deal of good. Damien had tried to tell her more with his body, lips, hands, than he could bring himself to say in words. She knew that he had cared to some extent; he had demonstrated that with the pain he had exhibited when she told him that she would no longer see him.

She wished wistfully that they could still be friends, for she valued him highly as a person. She wanted to see him again. She wanted to watch a smile break over his dark face, like sunshine spilling over a hill. She wanted to tell him that she loved him and it was too late.

Her first feeling of lightheartedness, which was a usual experience for her when she started off on a trip, dissipated to a tired depression. Light was fading fast and she realised with some annoyance that she had underestimated the amount of time the car drive would take. She should either get a motel room for the night and call her father, or keep on. Impatient by nature, she shrugged irritably and decided to keep on driving.

Stopping at a motel would only be lonely and unsatisfying anyway, she told herself. Soon she had to switch on her headlights and concentrate more on her driving in the darkness. At least she had crossed the Vermont State border some time back.

She was just pulling out of a small town's city limit, accelerating with the higher speed limits posted and her mind ahead to the warm bed and welcome she would be receiving from her father when the small dog ran out in front of her car. Sheer exhaustion must have been what had dulled her senses so, because she normally had a very fast reaction time. Though tired and a bit slower than she normally would have been, she reacted almost instantly, ripping her steering wheel sharply around to slew the car to the right, heading off the road. She had just that split second to congratulate herself for turning right instead of left into the path of the oncoming car when she saw in her glaring headlights that the confused and frightened dog, which she now saw to be no more than a puppy, in an effort to jump out of the way had jumped right into the path of her car again. In that moment, she saw what she had not noticed before. She saw the sharp decline, the bank that she would hit and undoubtedly roll down if she were to swerve any more to the right. And she saw that with that split second's hesitation she had lost her chance to jerk the car's wheel left enough to avoid hitting the small dog and avoid flipping over. And because of the speed she was travelling at, she could not brake. It was either the embankment or the small, shivering puppy that was now frozen with terror.

She didn't even consider that a choice.

Oh, boy, she thought grimly, hitting the edge of the bank with a bump that sounded like it had broken something underneath, this is it. This is really it. God, help me get through this, help me live through this, oh, my dear God! 'Damien, I love you!'

The car plummeted, and went into a roll, and then another. She was thrown violently from one side to the next, as if she were in a crazy carnival ride from her childhood days, and her purse, suitcases, and map went flying all over in a weird, haphazard way. The most terrifying sound in the world came to her then, as an almighty crunching metallic scream rent her eardrums, and then she realised that she was screaming too. Something flew up and hit her face as the windshield shattered, and the car tilted one more time to come to a gentle rest on the driver's side, headlights still shining and engine stubbornly coughing. With a nightmare vision of the car exploding into flames, she reached out a violently shaking hand to turn the ignition key off, and the coughing engine subsided.

She was lying on her side and staring out into a black and green night with deep black shadows thrown up by her glaring headlights. She looked down at the ground, twisting her head a little, and saw torn grass sprinkled over with sparkling shards of glass. She was wrapped in a tangled, ruined piece of metal machinery, with glass, pencils, and clothes flung all over the place. Part of her road map rested crazily on her head like a hat, which was nice because liquid was trickling down the side of her cheek and she wanted to cover up so that the rain wouldn't soak her through, and that was very strange because it must have just started raining. She didn't remember it raining before. She reached up one tentative hand, touched her face, and it felt sticky. That wasn't rain. It was blood. With a sudden, horrified, delayed reaction, she jerked her body hard in an effort to get loose and escape the nightmare, to get out of the crumpled, frightening metal that had once been such a nice safe car, and she couldn't move out. She was trapped, in the middle of the night, and would probably die before morning from some kind of internal injury.

Jessica had never really considered her own death before, and right now she was realising how very possible it would be for her to just go to sleep right here and never see anyone again. She sobbed out a scream of pure terror and pain, just one, and then heard the far off shouts. Someone was yelling loud enough to wake the dead, and that wasn't very funny, Jessica, she told herself sternly, but really, that fellow had a nice pair of lungs on him.

The other car! She had forgotten about the other car! Someone was there and had seen the whole thing, and she would be helped in just a minute, just a few minutes, and all she had to do was to hold on to her sanity and not give way to a bout of screaming hysteria, and everything would be all right, but first she rather thought that a nice nap would be just the thing to make her feel better. . . . She'd just close her eyes for a few minutes and then Damien would come and save her. She'd just close her eyes for one second. Just one.

She was out cold when gentle hands extricated her from the two tons of twisted metal. She didn't feel a thing when she was set carefully on an ambulance stretcher and carried very gently up the hill she had so precipitously descended. She didn't hear the wailing, urgent sirens that cleared the path for her trip to the emergency room at the local hospital. She didn't feel the administering, professional hands that tended her. She slept a long time.

Voices penetrated the fog that surrounded Jessica's tired brain, and she eventually recognised one of them as belonging to her father. But they were so loud, and interrupting her sleep, and didn't they have any idea of how lousy she felt? She needed her rest. Without opening her eyes, she said clearly, 'Shut up, will you? Let a girl get her sleep, already.' The voices stopped as if she had startled them and then someone laughed. A gentle touch was then laid on her cheek for a moment, and she realised that someone had just kissed her. 'Hi, Dad,' she whispered, starting to go under the sedation again.

'Hello, sweetheart. Get some rest and we'll talk later, okay?' She wanted to open her eyes and look at him, but couldn't seem to move her muscles right.

'Okay. I messed the car up, didn't I?'

'You certainly did. It's a miracle that you weren't hurt more than you were. Now be quiet and sleep, all right?'

But she had to ask one more question, and it was too important to wait, so with an effort she forced her eyes open to stare at her father's lined, loving face. 'Did I hurt the dog, Daddy?'

His face softened with understanding. 'No, precious, you missed him completely. Now shut up and sleep, will you?'

She mouthed, 'Tyrant,' and watched him smile before drifting off. She felt her fingers taken and held, and that was the last thing she knew for a long time.

Her stay at the hospital ended up being relatively short. When she finally woke up, it was well into the next day, and her father had left to eat supper. She felt strangely weak and was quite content to close her eyes and drift. Her entire body hurt, as if someone had taken a ton of bricks and dumped the whole lot right on top of her and then jumped up and down on the pile for good measure. Her face was bandaged on her right side, above her eye and gauze was wrapped around her head. She wondered what the bandaging covered.

She found out the next day, when the doctor paid her a quick visit to check her over. He was a slight, grey-haired, bristly fellow with fierce, merry eyes. He sat down beside her on the bed and frowned deeply into her eyes. 'I heard that you got up this morning, disobeying my strict orders to stay in bed,' he accused, switching on a light and peering into her left pupil.

She grinned. 'I had to go to the bathroom and didn't fancy using a bed pan, thank you very much. There was no harm done.'

He snorted. 'Well, since you went ahead and did it, how did you feel? Weak, or dizzy? Were you sick to your stomach?' He turned the light to her right pupil.

'Nope. I was a little shaky, and my right leg is very bruised, but other than a slight headache, I feel fine.'

He sat back and looked at her carefully. 'Did your father tell you that we were keeping you for observation since you had received a nasty bump on the head?'

'Yes.' She raised her own unbandaged brow at him expectantly.

'You're doing just fine. There's no concussion, and the only real damage appears to be to your face. You do realise that you're going to be scarred?'

Jessica frowned, feeling alarmed. 'I—expected as much. I remember the glass flying out and hitting me. How—how badly will it be?' The last was asked with a degree of apprehension that he hastened to reassure.

'It isn't terrible, so don't start to worry that you are going to look like a freak, or anything foolish like that. But it will definitely be noticeable, I'm afraid, and will need corrective surgery if you are to go back to modelling? That's right, isn't it—you are a model?'

'Yes, I am,' she murmured, shaken. 'What is it going to look like?'

'You were cut from above your eyebrow right about there to down your temple and hitting the cheekbone. It was nasty, and it disappears into your hairline, but fortunately not far, so we didn't have to shave any hair away. It needed quite a few stitches. Like I said, after a few months, after it's had a chance to heal up some, you can receive corrective surgery and with cosmetics, I'm sure that it won't be visible to the naked eye. You were fortunate that your bone structure was not damaged. You won't have as much muscle control as you had previously, because of nerve damage and scar tissue, and you will probably feel a bit numb around your right brow bone. Some of that won't ever go away. But it will be negligible. It'll make your frowns a little lopsided and your one eyebrow shoot up higher than the other one, nothing much. And of course, you don't frown for pictures, do you?'

She had to laugh at that, partly from relief and partly from trying to imagine herself frowning lopsidedly at the camera in a modelling pose. 'Can I have a mirror?'

'It wouldn't be wise,' he replied immediately. 'You've a very bruised face and it looks awful. Give it time for the funny colours to subside before you take a peek. Other than that, I can't see any reason for us to keep you any longer, unless you like the food here.'

She laughed again and shook her head, and it felt strangely heavy on the one side with all of the bandages. 'I can't say as I do, doctor. What should I do about the stitches?'

'Nothing for about two weeks. You can give me a call then and make an appointment to get them removed, or you can get your own physician to take them out, if you like. And like I said, give yourself time to heal up, okay?'

'All right. Thank you.'

CHAPTER SIX

JESSICA was shocked, as she stared out at the mangled mess of metal that sat in a lot beside the local tow truck and garage. She turned large eyes towards her father and exclaimed, 'And I lived through that?'

Will King surveyed his daughter's bruised face seriously, gently. 'And you lived through that. Makes you feel grateful, doesn't it?'

She nodded slowly, turning her gaze back as if compelled, to the wreckage. 'I'm just glad to be alive and walking around after that. It's a miracle that I didn't even have anything broken!' After a few moments, she made a real effort to overthrow her mood and said lightly, 'And let's hope that little mutt appreciates it, too! I sure hope his owner teaches him not to run out in the road. Well, I guess it's a good thing I have the insurance to cover it, huh?'

'What, the mutt?'

'Silly. The car, of course.' She turned her face determinedly away from the ruined car. 'We might as well go. There's nothing for us here.'

The rest of the drive to Rutland was completed in almost total silence for she dozed most of the way and her father let her sleep. By the time she had her things tucked away in her bedroom in her father's small, painfully tidy house, she was feeling as if she had run a marathon. Sweat made her blouse stick to her back and she gingerly lowered herself into an easy chair in the living room, just in front of an empty fireplace, groaning in agony. 'My right leg is so bruised and stiff, I can hardly bear to move it!'

Will looked up with a frown. He had been studying a wildlife and field guide, and he laid the book aside. 'I noticed that you were limping. Nothing serious, I hope? I can't remember the doctor mentioning it.'

She shook her head and the fiery glints in her hair caught her father's attention briefly. 'No, it's just banged up pretty badly! I whacked it on the gear shift. It ought to loosen up as I use it more.'

Will looked down at his hands and said carefully, 'I'm sorry about your face, Jess, honey. Will it make a difference to your career?'

She reached up a hand and touched the bandage that covered one side of her face. 'Yes, it'll just about ruin it, I imagine,' she said cheerfully, and caught her father's wince. 'Oh, Daddy, don't worry about it! Really! If I wanted to, I could have plastic surgery and be just about the same, but I don't know if I want to go to the trouble and expense for just another seven years or so left to my modelling career.'

'Your modelling could pay the hospital bills within a year and you know it,' he returned, looking puzzled. 'Let alone what insurance would pay. Your earning power as a model is fantastic, Jess. Expense can't be the reason, surely?'

'Well, no, it isn't,' she admitted, after a short silence. 'I just don't know if I want to go back to modelling or not, Dad. I wanted to come up here to think things through, I guess. And if I don't go back, then there's no reason to worry about a stupid scar, is there?' She shook herself out of her reverie and laughed at him. 'Besides, it might add an air of mystery and adventure to me! Men are going to flock to my side, fall in love with my wonderful air and spend their time guessing at my sordid past!'

Her father had to chuckle at that. 'You nut, that's

what women are supposed to do to men who have been scarred in a duel.'

'Sexist,' she replied, without any heat. 'Surely it should work the other way around? Hey, I'm starved, aren't you? No? Well, I'm going to fix myself an omlette and if you want some you're welcome to it.'

He looked amused at that, his lined face crinkling in a way that was as familiar to her as breathing. 'I thought you didn't cook anymore, Miss High Society.'

She looked like a guilty criminal caught in the middle of a crime as she stood up, slim and tall, her right leg stiff. She massaged it as she whispered dramatically, 'Sh, don't tell anyone! I occasionally stretch my talents to include an odd omelette or two, but if word leaks out, then my reputation is ruined!'

'As I remember,' Will said reminiscently, 'your omelettes were pretty odd. No, thank you, I may have some soup later.'

She smiled down at him and impulsively bent to kiss his cheek. 'I'm sorry that I worried you, Dad.'

He reached up and patted her discoloured cheek. 'Why, honey, you couldn't help it. And you're all right, so everything worked out in the end.'

She went and limped on into the kitchen. Moving slowly and awkwardly because of her bad leg, she had time to reflect on her conversation with her father. She had been doing a lot of thinking and she really didn't think she wanted the surgery. She had been getting tired of the outward perfection of her face and body that seemed to attract people to her for the wrong reasons. She had mulled over the conversation that she had some weeks ago with Justin. She had said that people wanted her for her pretty packaging, and they didn't know the real her, the person that could be housed in any kind of flesh. She thought that she would rather like to put that to the test.

She was tired of being a perfect, plastic doll, and the scar seemed to symbolise that. Who knows? When she got the bandage off and looked at herself in the mirror she might be genuinely horrified and want the plastic surgery anyway. But somehow she doubted it.

Something was changing inside her, something that had been thrust into motion by the catalyst of her break-up with Damien, and she was content to flow with whatever tide was sweeping her into a different life.

The days fell into a gentle, undemanding pattern for her and her father. She rested at first, content to read and relax while her face and leg finished the healing process. Then she started to spend time in her father's bookshop, helping out in a clumsy way and laughing at her own mistakes, and generally just having a good time with her dad. Still, for all of her apparent light-heartedness, Will caught the creases of pain around her eyes and mouth at odd times, when she thought she wasn't being observed and though he didn't say anything to her, he wondered.

She didn't wear any make-up during the two weeks and avoided looking in the mirror, and gradually she became more easy in her movements, both in comfort and in natural posing. The modelling pose that she had once adopted constantly fell away, and she even slouched in an easy chair when she felt like it. Her hair went loose and free, no longer put up in the smooth, elegant chignon all of the time, and she lost that stark thinness, acquiring a faint curve to her breasts and hips again.

She didn't talk about personal matters, and Will also noticed this and wondered.

When they made the trip to the local doctor to have

her stitches removed, she refused to look into a mirror until they had returned back home and she was up in the privacy of her own room. Then, heart pounding with a fear that she both acknowledged and cursed impatiently, she looked slowly into her dressing-table mirror fully for the first time in several weeks.

At first the angry red, healing scar was a definite shock, but then as she became used to it and the fact that the redness would soon fade, a strange smile curved her perfect lips. The vision reflected in the mirror was at once incongruous and yet somehow symbolic. The perfection of the face and that one, single stroke that marred the marble smooth quality to her skin was all indicative of what she was inside. She wasn't perfect, calm, or even totally reasonable inside, and she had played that role too long to want to go back to it now. There was another beauty that she was beginning to learn: the beauty of naturalism.

And so for the most part she was making what she deemed progress in the renovation of her self, both physically and mentally. But, oh, how she missed Damien.

She liked to hold imaginary conversations with him, as if he were really there, with her, holding her hand. It was a painful exercise and yet rather fun, to daydream that they were married and he would never leave her again, that he was somehow calmer inside himself and ready to settle in one place. It was a nice dream. And it was too bad that it was only a dream.

She supposed resignedly that she would love him for the rest of her life. For all of her changes in her body and mind, that one factor remained as steady as the core of her self. Could she ever give up his memory in order to marry someone else? That was the question that she pondered early one evening as she slouched alone in her favourite easy chair, the lights in the living room off and music from the stereo filling the house with the essence of its sound. The outside light from the porch shone in the front picture window and illuminated things well enough. A fire helped also and threw heat on her outstretched toes. She cradled a drink in her hands, sank her chin into her chest and thought.

He would be right behind her. He would be almost within touching distance and he would ask her how she was and she would reply mildly, oh, fine and then they would talk over the good times and the bad times and she wouldn't feel anything for him except for a sad vague, well-it-was-good sort of feeling. No, that's not true. If he were standing right behind her, she would be swamped with such a feeling of love and longing she would probably throw herself right at him and fling her arms around his waist.

She was so wrapped up in her daydreams, so intent on herself, that she never heard the soft even footsteps out on the front porch. Her father was not coming back until fairly late, for he was playing cards with old friends, and she wasn't expecting anyone to call. She never noticed when the door opened up and the footsteps came up to stop right behind her.

When Damien spoke, it was such a natural extension of her daydream that she never even jumped. 'Jess?'

She took a sip of her drink. Funny, she seemed to have known from the beginning that he would be here tonight. 'Hello, Damien.'

There was a pause. She didn't jump up to throw her arms around him, nor did she feel as passively as she might have wished. Instead, a warm steady glow filled her up inside, as if a fire had been started in a hearth that had for too long been empty.

Then that low gentle voice said, 'May I sit down?'

She stirred then, turned her eyes up and smiled at his big black silhouette. 'Of course. Did I leave the front door unlocked again?'

'Yes. Don't bother getting up—I locked it behind me.' He walked over to the other easy chair to her left, and sat down. With the darkness pervading the corners of the room and the flickering red and yellow hues from the fireplace, he seemed to be a creature of the night and of fire, rippling warm colour dancing on his dark skin, making his eyes brilliant, putting gleams of red in his dark hair and sending half of his face into blackness.

She had to smile again. 'Tell me, Damien, are you really Mephistopheles? Here I sit, all alone, staring at a fire in the night, thinking of you, and you magically appear.'

He stirred, turning his gaze to the flames, sighing. 'No, Jess. I'm only a man. Why did you run away from New York?'

She brooded at that, tucking in her chin again and looking down at her glass, her hair falling over her face in a concealing cloud. 'Tell me, why did you follow me here?'

Silence. The sound of flaming tongues licking hungrily at dry wood, crackling, snapping. She hadn't expected an answer to her question and so when he did speak, she jumped, as violently as she should have when he had come up behind her. 'To see you, to talk to you. I've missed you, Jessie.'

She whispered an instant response, 'I've missed you, too.' Firelight flickering, it was so warm and comforting and real. She didn't have a fireplace in her apartment. She really needed to move, to find some place that suited her better. A joyful, painful feeling welled up in her, welled up and spilled out, all over the carpet and the reflections of the dancing flames licked at it, absorbing. 'Hey, look, I can't take any more confrontations. I really would like it if you just went away, Damien,' she said softly, closing her eyes. 'Go away. Please! Go back. I'm trying to be good here and trying to build another life, and you're going to wreck it all and make me unhappy with what I've got. Damien, don't hurt me—just go home, okay?'

That black and red, strong, still figure galvanised into action. He catapulted forward, thrust out of his seat by his two quick hands, and then he was kneeling in front of her chair, holding her hands tightly, resting his head on her knees. She was so incredibly shaken, so completely taken aback, that all she could do was instinctively to bend over his dark head, her hair falling like rain over both of their faces, flamelike, and she pressed her forehead to his hair.

'The last thing I'd ever want to do to you is hurt you,' he whispered. 'That's the last thing I ever intended! Oh, why did everything have to go wrong? Jessie, why couldn't you stay?'

She just rested, and the warm, tight hold he had on her hands felt so exquisitely wonderful that the pain in her heart threatened to break down her resolve. 'Darling, I just wasn't handling my life. I—nothing was right, and I just didn't want to live a sterile life anymore!'

He spoke, and she felt the movement of his lips through her slacks. 'Will you marry me? Please, Jess, will you marry me?'

Her head jerked up and she stared down at his bent head, shocked. At one time she had thought he would never say those words to any woman. And, at one time she had thought he was going to say those words to someone else. Then a sad smile tugged at her lips. 'Did Mary say no?'

He held very still. 'I never asked her. It was wrong from the very beginning and you knew it. You are a very wise lady. Even as you helped that little sweet thing to become the prettiest and the most attractive she could be, you must have known all along. Was it your way of showing me just how young she really was, by giving her all of that glamour and glitter?'

She had to laugh. 'I don't know. I think I hoped so, in a way, although Mary certainly figured in it largely. She wanted it so badly, you know. I wonder if she will find it all that she had dreamt it to be. But yes, I think I did hope to show you that the package is not what mattered, and if you happened to fall in love with the new Mary Mouse, when you didn't so much as look at the old one, why then I guess I wished you two all of the happiness in the world. She never really changed on the inside, though, except maybe to think better of herself.'

'And you would never have respected me again in your life.' There was a smile in his voice, that rueful, quizzical tone she knew so well and welcomed, and she laughed again, squeezing the hands holding hers. Ice chinked and she automatically pressed her half-finished drink into his hand. As automatically, he settled at her feet and drank. Ice chinked again, a light, silvery sound, and then he handed the glass back to her. 'You never answered my question, darling.'

'And you always did press for an immediate answer,' she returned quietly, trying to avoid the issue. He didn't pressure her. 'How in the world did you know where to find me, anyway? The only person I told was ... oh, no. You didn't go and see Justin, did you?'

'Yes, I did, and had a devil of a time tracking the fellow down, too. He's not listed in the phone book, and I had no idea where he lived.'

'What did you do?' She took a sip of her drink and closed her eyes. Strange, how relaxing it was just to be with him, to just love him, even though nothing had been resolved, even though she knew he did not love her.

'I went to court.'

'Oh, no!' Her eyes flew open and she stared at him in consternation. 'You actually bothered him in court? What—what happened?'

'I told him I wanted to talk to him, he gave me his phone number, we got together and talked. Yes, contrary to popular belief, I did not smash his blond, handsome face in, and he did not retaliate in kind. We were very civil. He's a good friend for you. He really cares.'

She stared down at him in amazement, feeling his fingers play idly with hers. 'I know that. I'm just a bit surprised to hear you admit it, that's all. Damien, do you feel all right?'

'No.' He turned his head, a neat, swift movement, and tried to see her expression in the semi-darkness. 'I'm lonely, and at night my bed is cold and empty.' She jerked at that admission; he was not seeing anyone else. His fingers tightened on hers. 'Jessica, please answer me. Will you marry me?'

Her heart thudded, raced, roared, and her lips shook. Here was her chance, right here was her big chance, don't blow it, baby, don't blow it now, he'll never offer again. 'No,' she whispered, and felt sick.

His fingers stilled, slackened. 'Why not?' It was a whispered question, like her answer had been, low, intense, almost angry.

'Oh, dear Damien,' she half moaned, reaching out to stroke his head with a gentle, slightly shaking hand. 'I don't know if I can make you understand. I—I'm not very good at explaining my emotions.'

His tone, after that first shocked response, was under control, dry. 'I know. I'm only now beginning to see how much you've kept inside you. I'll listen, if you care to try, darling.'

Her hand stilled on his head. 'Where do I start? I don't know when it all started to go sour, even now I don't know. And I'm not necessarily talking about you, I'm talking about my whole life, which you incidentally happened to be a part of.' She felt him relax. He was vulnerable, yes, after all, her Damien was vulnerable. It was a revelation all over again. She had the power to hurt him, how deeply, she didn't know, but he did care enough so that she could hurt him. She was touched.

'What went sour on you?'

'Everything. Oh, this last decade has been quite a time, I can tell you. I started out, so full of goals and hopes and dreams! And the climb in the business was fun, wasn't it? I worked, and I sweated, and I dragged myself to the top. I was good. I was good! You know that, you had as much fun watching me climb as I did working to get there. It was the intangible, the unattainable that somehow I was going to attain. Nobody tells you how flat the mountaintop can be after getting there. Everything just went stale. There's only so many smiles and so many poses that can be practised in front of a camera, and I did them all, didn't I? At least I had the decency to keep my clothes on; I didn't go that far, and never will! But I was bored with everything. And then of course, I didn't feel like I was getting what I needed out of our relationship.'

He stirred. 'What do you feel you needed out of our relationship?'

Love. Support. Comfort. Fidelity. Love. She sighed. 'It doesn't matter what I thought I needed. It's just that I wasn't getting it. What does matter is that I'm not going back to that life, or to our relationship again.'

'Relationships change. You are giving up for points that could very well be irrelevant,' he said, a thread of impatience beginning to shoot through his voice.

'Do you want me to spell every little thing out for you?' she asked, starting to get angry at how he was pushing her into a corner. 'Yes, I can see that you do, the same old Damien. I don't want to get back together with you because—because, dammit, you can make me feel such rage at times, and it's a destructive, corrosive emotion that not only tears away at my insides but tears at you when I can't leash it! I—I was a sterile doll back in New York for too long, in an effort to control that rage, and I only managed to bottle everything up until it blew out all over the place! And it wasn't you, but it was everything in my life that I was angry at, and dissatisfied with, and I tried to make myself believe that I was happy because I felt that I should be happy with what I had!' And I felt rage at you, because you didn't love me the way I loved you, she added silently, furiously, and knew the words would never be spoken. Damien wouldn't, couldn't love a woman. How many times had he assured her of that? He did not love her the way she loved him. He could not. Damn him to hell, he could not. She crumpled in her chair suddenly. 'And I'm sorry, darling. It just wouldn't work. I'd be too afraid of hurting both myself and you, and of all the people in the world, we are the two I'd hate to hurt the most!' He half-laughed at that, shaking his head.

'You're wrong.'

She stirred. 'What d'you mean?'

'Just what I said: you are wrong. About a lot of things, but we won't go into that now, it's pretty late, and I expect you're tired. I will tell you this, though: I fully intend marrying you, sooner or later. We'd suit in so many ways, and I find I really do want this to work.

Resign yourself, darling.' She shook her head, amazed at his arrogance. He stood and stretched a little. 'How about one more drink? I think I could use something a little more substantial than what you had in your glass . . . over here? I'll just flip on the light for a moment, so guard your eyes.' The light came on and flooded the room with a brightness that after the warm, cosy glow of the fire made her blink.

She yawned, tiredly thinking that after this drink she would have to find some way to convince him to go back to the world he came from. How could she convince him that she no longer wanted what her old world had to offer? How could she tell him that she could not be happy living that kind of lifestyle anymore? How did she know, herself? She let her head fall back against the back of the chair, her dark red hair falling away from a nearly pure profile, a profile that would never again be as pure as it once had been.

He had walked over to the cabinet and had poured himself a brandy. She could have placed a bet on the drink; that's how well she knew his likes and dislikes. He turned, looked over one wide shoulder and asked her, 'Would you like for me to freshen you—My God!'

That sharp, shocked voice jerked her head up and she stared at him with wide eyes, one brow drawing to her perfect nose, the other stationary. She could feel it, could feel the tug of the contractable muscles on the left in comparison to the immovable numbness on her right, and realisation and memory flooded through her at the horrified look on his face. She groaned once, a deep sound of pain, and put up her hands to cover her face. 'Oh no, I forgot, I completely forgot all about it!'

Her vision went dark, because of the fingers covering her eyes, and she had just enough time to notice the red outline of her fingers' blood vessels as the light penetrated between them, something she had always noticed as a child, and then her hands were jerked away and Damien, eyes carrying that awful shocked look, came close to run his gaze over her scarred face. She felt acutely self-conscious, so much so that she twisted and turned in an effort to get away from his eyes, but he grabbed her head and held her still as he looked his fill on her face.

Futile, stupid, irrational tears filled her eyes and she finally stopped trying to move away from his gaze but met his eyes head on, her eyes glittering brilliantly, hugely.

'Your face,' he said in a kind of moan, 'What happened to your beautiful face? How did this happen to you? When—how, answer me!' In his agitation, he took her by the shoulders and gave her a quick hard shake.

The tears spilled over and she said, sobbing, 'An accident, I had an accident. I—I went off the road trying to miss a puppy and my car rolled down an embankment. The windshield shattered.' She went mute, just staring at him. Did it really matter so much to him, that scar? Did he really care about such things after all? She started to go numb, because she didn't want to think about it.

'Oh, my God!' he breathed, hauling her close to wrap his arms hard around her. 'You could have been killed, you could have died weeks ago, I would never have known!' He backed up, looked down at her again, and something like pity flitted across his face. She saw it and was horrified. Then he was saying gently, 'It doesn't look irreparable, darling. We can get it fixed up, and I'm sure you could model again. You needn't let this stand in your way after all, don't you see?'

She surged to her feet, knocking his hands away from

her, appalled. 'No, by God! I will not! Oh, Damien, you're just as bad as all the rest are, you only care for the outside, but you don't care for me, for *me*! That's all everyone's been telling me, get it fixed, get it taken care of—is it so hellish to look at? Is it so damned ugly to you? Well, that's just tough, that's really tough, because if you don't like it, then you can take a leaping jump off somewhere! Do you know what? I *like it*! I'm not a plastic doll anymore, I'm a human being again! I'm not a business investment, I'm a person with feelings that you've just jumped all over and trampled on, dammit!' She was in a rage now and totally out of control, and she whirled to rush away from him as if the proximity of his body was too much for her.

Then she turned at the other end of the room, dark, red hair flying out, eyes glowing molten fire, and the look of rage on her face together with the scar above her brow, made her look more anguished than she could know.

'No, Jessica!' Damien was white, his eyes burning, and he came after her quickly. 'That's not what I meant! I just thought that you were trying to reconcile yourself to the loss of your career by all of your talk before, and you don't have to leave it all if you don't want to—that's all I was trying to say!'

She gave vent to her frustration by putting her two clenched hands against her head and snarling through gritted teeth. 'Then will you just listen to me for a minute? Will you pay attention to what I'm saying? Read my lips, if you have to! I left. Town. Because I didn't. Want to live. That life, anymore! The accident didn't matter to me! But I can see it obviously matters to you!'

'Yes, it matters to me!' he bellowed out, his powerful voice shaking through the house. 'By the sound of it, you damn near died out there, and that matters to me!'

Feeling hurt and wanting to lash out because of that hurt, she jeered mockingly, 'And the scar matters to you, doesn't it? Huh, doesn't it?'

'Yes!' he shouted, goaded by her attitude. 'That damned scar matters to me! Whenever you're hurt it matters to me! Woman, will you just calm down a minute and listen to reason?'

'What is it?' she cried out, knocking against a nearby table and sending an ash tray crashing to the floor. 'Am I too ugly for you now? Well that's just too bad, mister! If I'm not good enough for you, take it somewhere else!' She turned and eyed him with her too-brilliant eyes, feeling as if the top of her head were about to split apart. 'Is that really why you didn't ask poor Mary Mouse to marry you? Even all dolled up she wasn't good enough, was she?'

'Shut up, Jessica!' he snarled, looking incredibly dangerous. 'You are going to push me too far, so just shut up!'

'Tell me,' she said suddenly, staring at him so fiercely and so hurt. 'If I had looked like Mary, would you have looked twice at me? Would you? *Would you?*'

'No!' He was over to her in two strides and had a hold on her jaw, making her stare right back at him. He was so angry! He was so deep into his anger he didn't realise how badly he was hurting her. 'I would not have given you a second look, not so much as a single thought if you hadn't been as beautiful as you were! What the hell is the matter with that? You knew I found you attractive from the beginning! You found me attractive, admit it! Come on now, I want you to admit it like you made me—you liked how I looked!'

She stared at him bitterly, hatefully. 'Yes!' she spat,

furious at having to admit it. 'Yes, I did! But if I had it to do again, I'd have run as fast as I could in the other direction!'

His eyes narrowed and he let go of her jaw so fast she nearly unbalanced and fell. 'Well,' he said, backing up a few paces, 'now we know, don't we?'

'Yes,' she burst out, anxious to try and send him as far away as possible from her, so that she could go and lick her wounds in private. 'And you might as well give up any notion of getting me to have plastic surgery, because I just won't do it! And if you don't like the looks of it, then you just go back to New York and find someone else that suits your idea of beauty! I won't play that game anymore, not for you or for anyone else, so just get out of here, will you?'

She turned her back to him, crossed her arms around herself and waited to hear his footsteps taking him out that door and out of her life, again. One part of herself was appalled at how she had ripped up at him and the other part was appalled that he should think so much of her looks. She just couldn't live with him anyway, so it was a good thing he was going to leave. When they got into a fight, they had one mother and father of a fight, and not only did they manage to hurt each other pretty well, but they managed to wreck their surroundings like twin tornadoes cutting a path of destruction. She didn't want that kind of destructiveness in her life.

There was complete silence from behind her, not even footsteps sounding to the door. She was going crazy at the silence, when she heard a car door slam outside and she groaned deep in her throat. That was Dad back from playing cards and now she would have to introduce Damien to him, and to try to pretend to a politeness that neither she nor Damien would be feeling, and how was she going to act normal after such a cataclysmic argument?

She turned and hissed at Damien's back, since he'd turned at the car door slamming. Even while she spoke to him angrily, she ran her eyes down the elegant, masculine lines of his body appreciatively. 'Now see what you've done? You should have got out of here before. That's my father!'

He turned slowly, brandy glass in hand and lean face, incredibly, calm and even amused. She noted it; he had time to get himself calm while she had been fighting with her own emotions. She had to stare. She was as taut as a bowstring after their yelling match, and he looked almost relaxed, and that, on top of everything, made her angry too. 'Well, I can see you're adept at masking your emotions!' she snapped and nearly threw something at him when he laughed.

He replied calmly, 'Get yourself together, darling. We've got to act normal for your father, and we can argue this all out later.'

She stamped her foot, a childish, useless burst of bad temper. 'We will not!'

He just looked at her, as the front door opened to admit Will. 'Yes, Jessica, we will.'

CHAPTER SEVEN

WILL entered the living room and looked with interest at the tall, darkly, good-looking man who stood facing his daughter, a drink of brandy held in one negligent, long-fingered hand. 'Hello, there,' he said, striding forward to hold out a hand. It was clasped, briefly and with a grip so hard he wanted to wince. A nice grip, he decided. 'I'm Jessie's father, Will.'

'Damien Kent. How do you do?' The two men sized each other up and each liked what he saw. 'I thought I was the only one who called her Jessie.'

She watched the two men she had wanted to keep apart, and her foot began to unconsciously tap out a rapid staccato on the rug. Damien turned on the charm and her father, she could see, was falling for it. He liked the younger man. Well, it was just too bad since everything was falling into a shambles around her and now Damien and she would never be together again. Her one eyebrow lifted, sardonically, and her mouth pursed.

Will turned back to his daughter and was inwardly very interested indeed. He had not seen her so close to the edge of her control since she had been a young, undisciplined, spirited girl. In fact, he had begun to wonder at her phenomenal calm as the days had gone by and she did not so much as throw a cooking pan. That, for Jessica, was very unusual. And here she was, nearly dancing with temper, and he would lay odds with anyone that it was all because of the large fellow in front of him now. His grizzled grey brows rose in surprise and the beginnings of a smile flitted across his creased face. So that was the lay of the land! 'We decided to quit early tonight, dear. Gareth has a nasty cough.'

'That's too bad,' she murmured, gritting her teeth at the stupid, unnecessary small talk. 'Maybe I can call on him tomorrow. In the meantime, it's getting pretty late and Damien was just going, weren't you, darling?'

Will asked him, 'Did you drive all the way from New York today?' And Damien, damn him, was answering in the affirmative, his dark eyes dancing to hers wickedly. 'Well you certainly can't be planning to make the return trip tonight, are you?'

'No,' that devil replied, leaning at his ease against the side of the comfortable sofa, whirling the drink in his glass gently. 'I was thinking of checking into a motel room, if there's still one open.'

Jessica's brow lowered ominously and she started to see red. If there was still one open! What was he playing at, for heaven's sake? Of course there were motels open at this time of night! Then her father was speaking and she could barely believe what she was hearing.

'Well, there's certainly no reason for you to stay at a motel when we have several rooms unoccupied right here, is there?' He looked over at his daughter and nearly laughed aloud. 'Isn't that right, Jessie?'

'Why, Father, if he wants to stay at a motel, I don't see why we should try to persuade him otherwise,' she replied, outwardly sweet but inwardly smouldering. The two men exchanged glances as if they understood each other perfectly, and this made her blood pressure rise perilously to the point of explosion.

'To tell the truth, I was not really looking forward to staying in a strange motel,' Damien said hesitantly, his lips quivering ever so slightly as he looked across the room at her. This, from a man who spent more time in other cities than in his own home, was just too much for her.

'That's the biggest pile of——' she began hotly, but was interrupted by her father.

'Jessica!' she was warned sternly, and she subsided to a mute glare at both of them. Will turned and said cordially, 'We'd be honoured to have you stay with us, at least for one night. You're welcome to stay as long as you like. Jessie, why don't you get the front guest room ready and I can help Mr Kent with his things.'

They both turned to the door and she heard Damien say smoothly, 'Please, call me Damien. All my friends do.'

'And of course my name is Will, and it's not short for William but for Wilfred, and I never could stand to be called that. . . .'

The front door slammed on the two talking men and she just stood for a moment, stunned at the unexpected turn of events the night had taken. Damien was actually staying for the night! He was going to be under the same roof as her, sleeping in a bed so close to her own, his naked relaxed body so near. . . . 'Damn it!' she cried out angrily, kicking out angrily and knocking over the small table she stood by.

The two men outside the door heard the thud and they looked at each other, Will's lined face creasing into a smile and Damien's eyes unfathomable in the dark shadows thrown by the overhead light. Then they both turned and continued their way to Damien's sleek car.

Jessica stomped up the stairs and yanked open the door to the guest room furiously. She stood for a moment, surveying the homely furnishings and the comfortable bed, thinking of Damien's own home which was the ultimate in elegant rich furnishings. He didn't belong here, didn't belong at all, and she suddenly got a vicious satisfaction out of thinking of his face when he saw the homemade rug, the scratched wood on the bed frame, and the plain-coloured, frilled curtains.

She went over to the dresser and pulled open the bottom drawer to take out the linen stored there. Then, with energetic, swift movements that helped her let off steam, she went to the bed, stripped off the covering blankets in one sweep, and began to tuck in the bottom sheet roughly.

'Here, let me help you with that,' a voice sounded behind her, and Damien walked in calmly, deposited his expensive leather bags, and brought his hands over hers. 'You can't be so rough with it and expect to have neat corners! I'll do this.'

And she watched with amazement as he calmly tucked in the corner sheet as if he had been doing it all his life. Then he stood and looked over the room with every sign of satisfaction. Her eyes nearly popped out of her head. 'How do you like your room?' she heard herself asking.

'Oh, it's very nice. The bed looks comfortable,' he replied, looking wickedly at her out of the corner of his eye. 'I should get a good night's sleep, don't you think? But I'd much rather have you with me, even if it meant getting no sleep at all. That kind of exhaustion can be very——'

'Shut up!' she hissed, thrusting herself away from him and his insinuations. She shot for the door and paused for a moment to look back, her eyes throwing daggers at him. He looked placid, and the arrows bounced off his steely hide. She felt goaded into saying to him emphatically, 'Don't you think this changes anything, mister, don't you get any bright ideas, do you hear? My door is locked, every night, for as long as you stay, and I will not, repeat not, in a million years marry you, so you might as well get back to New York as fast as you can!'

'I don't know,' he said mildly, and Damien being mild when she had just ripped up at him was another first in her experience, so she again stopped and stared. 'I've been wanting to take a vacation for quite some time now. Remember you and I talked about taking our vacations together? Well, it's been a few years and much too long, so I think I just might take your father up on his kind invitation. You surely wouldn't mind, would you, darling?'

Incensed, she swore and catapulted out of the room, and the sound of his truly amused laughter followed her down the hall, making her want to fall down and kick her heels against the floor in a screaming tantrum.

Smashing into her room with enough impetus to make her shoot on to her bed accompanied by a great creaking of bed springs, Jessica plucked up her pillow and thumped it on top of her head while she buried her face in the bedspread. Thus hidden in a childish, half-forgotten way she had once indulged in when the world became too much to handle, she gave vent to her pent-up feelings, sobbing quietly until the bedspread was sodden and warm. Then she just lay there, wishing Damien to all kinds of hell and wishing herself dead.

That caught her up short. She'd had a near brush with death, enough to know that her wish was nothing but a childish reaction and not a true death wish, and it had been terrible to even think such a thing. She felt ashamed of herself, and ashamed that she had cursed at Damien. He had got the notion that he would do quite well by marrying her and she knew by his nature how hard it was to change his mind once he had it set. And she had no doubt that he would want her to have plastic surgery and she wasn't going to have it! She wasn't going to have the surgery and she wouldn't marry Damien if he were the last man on earth. She once told Justin that she would never marry without love, and that still held true. Not only did she have to love the man she married but he would have to love her too, love her enough to give his life to her, to want her enough to exclude all others. Oh brother, she thought, as the tears welled up again. This crying is for the birds.

When the gentle hand descended on to her shoulder, she jumped a mile with the shock of it, and then started to curse fluently. She had totally forgotten that her bedroom door was open, and in the past it wouldn't have mattered, for her father respected her privacy greatly and would not intrude, so that meant it had to be Damien.

'Get out of here!' she cried, chokily, jerking her shoulder away from his warm hand. 'You weren't invited in, so beat it, will you?'

The weight that had descended on to the bed did not shift, and she rolled over suddenly, her gaze blurred, her look anguished. She blinked and the tears fell down her cheeks, and then she could see clearly, see the whiteness of Damien's face, the burning emotion in his eyes, the clenching muscle in his jaw. Her face crumpled and she suddenly flailed out with her hands to strike him on the shoulders, in an effort to hurt him as much as she was hurting inside. He didn't retaliate and didn't even resist, but instead held her by her shoulders as if supporting her, bearing her onslaught patiently, and this was so unlike him that she just collapsed into his arms, crying. She was enfolded tenderly, held carefully, and her own arms went around his neck convulsively as she buried her head in the hollow of his warm neck.

She was rocked and held and soothed until she felt finally in control of herself enough to loosen her hold on his neck and lean back. She smiled tentatively at him. He didn't smile back. 'I'm so sorry I hit you,' she offered quietly. 'There was no excuse for it, I know.'

His look didn't change. 'I'm sorry I hurt you. And I know that it was inexcusable, all that time, never giving a thought to your own emotional needs. I'm sorry, Jess. I'm sorry things weren't right.'

She searched herself for some feeling of surprise at this unexpected admission, and the only thing she felt surprise at was herself for taking his apology so calmly. The Damien she had known would have never admitted to doing wrong, but then the one observation that kept coming up and hitting her in the face was that this Damien had changed in some undefinable way. And from this new and unknown person, she could accept them.

She put up a slim hand and laid it against the side of his face as gently as she knew how, and she saw him close his eyes and swallow. 'I'm sorry too, darling. Because you know, it takes two to ruin a relationship, just as it takes two to make one. Don't castigate yourself. It was both of us, not just you.'

He gave a great sigh, opened his eyes, and was able to smile at her slightly. She saw the look in his eyes gradually return to normal, the self-accusation fading away, that strong visage coming into control. He searched her eyes intently and seemed to be satisfied with what he saw, for he nodded briefly. 'Good enough, for one evening, I suppose.'

'What do you mean?' she wanted to know, but he wouldn't answer that, merely shaking his head at her with a grin. She felt such a tide of love well up inside her at that gentle look that she nearly started to cry again. But, with an abrupt change of mood, she swung her legs off the bed and stood energetically. 'Well, I for one am starved! How about you?'

His eyes ran appreciatively over her figure. 'I think I could eat a chicken or two, or maybe three. It looks as though you've put on weight, darling.'

At that, she went over to the full-length mirror to stare at herself worriedly. 'Does it look bad?' Her eyes told her that it looked very good, the waist still long and slim, the breasts and hips slightly more rounded then they used to be, but she wanted to hear him say it.

'It looks fantastic,' he murmured, coming up behind her to put his hands heavily on her hips and draw her back against him. Their eyes met in the mirror. 'You look better now than I think I've ever seen you look. I know that the camera adds weight to the figure and that's why you always kept such a strict diet, but personally I prefer you like this.'

She said suddenly, bitterly, 'Scar and all?' and his light look melted away to a look of anger.

'That's enough about this particular subject,' he said evenly, after an obvious effort. 'We'll talk later, when we're both more calm.'

'I don't see why we should talk at all,' she snapped, jerking away from him to stalk to the door. 'As far as I'm concerned, case closed.'

He followed her closely and whispered into her ear, 'But you aren't the only one concerned, are you?'

Her head snapped around and she stared at him before continuing down the stairs without answering. She was afraid that she had come out of that exchange rather badly, and she hated not having the last word.

Down in the kitchen, she took stock of the refrigerator and started to pull out sandwich materials silently. If she had hoped to freeze him by her frosty attitude, she was sadly disappointed, for he brightened up once they were downstairs and began to talk lightly about various things. She felt incensed at the way he could apparently throw off his anger and feel so carefree, but gradually she began to listen to his words and not just his voice. Her own anger melted away as she became engrossed in what he was saying.

It was incredible. She had never heard him talk about his past before, except in the most general of terms, and here he was, calmly telling her about his childhood! She moved carefully to a chair and sat down, forgetting all about food as he talked.

'This is a nice house,' he said simply, looking around him uncritically. 'It's a lot nicer than where I grew up. Did your family live here, or did your father move in after your mother died?'

Jessica looked around and then returned her eyes to his face, blankly. With the eyes of love, this place was homely, comfortable, but certainly not pretty. The kitchen counter was scarred with countless knife marks, her father preferring to clean his fish inside, and the tiled floor was ancient and faded. The curtains in the windows were new and bright, but they clashed sadly with the colour of the old wallpaper. The refrigerator was as familiar to her as her own father, for her parents had bought it when she had been just a baby, and the ancient thing still obstinately worked.

She shook herself free of her observations and forced out an answer. 'Uh, yes, I've lived here all of my childhood. That's my old room upstairs that I'm in right now, and my old bed.'

'That's really nice. I'll bet you have good memories of this place,' he replied, tilting his head to look up at the ceiling, giving her an excellent view of his finely carved nostrils and firm jawline.

'I guess I do.'

'We lived in a two-room apartment. I had a brother and a sister, and my mom. My old man ran off when I was around two or so.' He still inspected the ceiling and so missed her look of shock.

After a bit she said carefully, 'I suppose it's rather hard to talk about it.' And she held her breath.

His head came down and he looked at her with brilliant black eyes, the emotion in them hard, somehow furious, convincing. 'When I got out of there, I told myself that I would never talk, think, or even try to remember back to those days. When I left, I wanted to put the whole nightmare behind me, to start completely anew and rebuild my life the way I wanted it to be. But it doesn't work that way, does it? We carry a little piece of our past with us throughout our entire lives.'

'I think that's true to a certain extent,' she replied, slowly. 'But it certainly shouldn't haunt us all of the time. We should learn from the past, value the lessons fate chooses to give to us, and then go on. The danger is when we try to totally erase the past and pretend it didn't exist. I guess that's why history tends to repeat itself and wars continually happen. It'd be nice, wouldn't it, if everyone would just wake up and realise what was happening in the world and that killing another person is about as heinous a crime that could be committed? Hell is for sinners, but war is a hell for the innocent, and it seems we never learn.'

His gaze softened on her face, the hardness in his eyes fading to another warmer emotion. 'Do you know something?' he said softly, and her eyes swivelled to his. 'You are really a wonderful and caring person. That splendid "packaging" as you so derisively put it, encases a splendid woman.'

'Do you want to make me blush?' she returned calmly, smiling at him as she experienced a feeling of *déj vu*. This was exactly like the many times she and Damien had talked over various subjects, and she was slipping into the old familiar pattern with an ominous ease. And yet, wasn't there a subtle difference?

She was different and so was he. She was no longer crippled by the fear of doing or saying something to send him away from her, and so she was more at ease with herself because of it. He was more willing to discuss feelings and emotions and moral issues that really mattered to them instead of trying to play some kind of intellectual game, making witty remarks and being terribly clever and never really touching the soul. The quality to their discussion was deeper, and she realised by the special look in his eyes that he knew it as well as she did.

She relaxed, sat back, and remembered the sandwiches. 'Good heavens, we've forgotten to eat! Well, I don't know about you, but I'm going to make myself a whopper of a sandwich . . . pass the mustard, will you? Thanks.'

Damien suddenly exclaimed, 'Good Lord!' And his hand shot out to grasp her wrist. She jumped, remembering how he had exclaimed with shock when he beheld her scarred face, and the same feeling of dread thudded in her chest. What was the matter? Then she saw that he was beginning to laugh and she relaxed slightly, still staring in puzzlement. 'Oh, Jess, I didn't mean to startle you. I'm sorry! It's just that I only now noticed that you haven't any fingernails! I can't remember ever seeing your nails unpainted, let alone short like that!'

She started to laugh too, her eyes bright and golden, her one brow slanting in a wicked-looking way, and her lips wide open in a generous smile that revealed dazzling white teeth. 'I broke several when the car rolled—I don't remember, but I must have tried to grab at the door or something. And then a few days ago I chipped some more when I did the dishes and it didn't seem very smart to keep half long and the other half short, so I cut them.'

His eyes widened exaggeratedly and he looked even more stunned as he whispered dramatically, 'You actually washed dishes?'

Her dismayed look, combined with the hand that flew to her mouth, had him laughing deeply all over again. 'Only once!' she cried, 'Only once! Don't breathe a word of it to anyone!' Then she was laughing too, and they both took their time in sobering up, reluctant to end the enjoyment of laughing together.

'Next you'll be telling me that you condescended to cook for your father!' he teased and then stared in honest astonishment as she looked embarrassed. 'No! Did you, really? Your father must rate pretty highly indeed. I don't think I ever managed to get you to fix me a home-cooked meal.'

'It was only once,' she protested, beginning to chuckle all over again. 'And I *hated* it—incidentally, so did my dad! Now he won't let me near the stove because he's afraid I'll serve him something rotten or poisoned, I think. So don't go thinking I've really changed that drastically. I couldn't cook something right if my life depended on it!'

'Some things never change,' he agreed, and then just looked at her, the light of amusement dying out of his eyes. She began to feel alarmed and hurriedly stood up.

'I think I'll just put everything away and go to bed now,' she said quickly, and as she turned her back to him she wondered at the look of dark fire that had been born in his eyes. She knew that look and had once welcomed it, but now it made her afraid, uneasy, and she wanted to escape.

She bent and put the sandwich materials in the refrigerator and as she stood up, she collided with his hard body right behind her. Shying away like a skittish colt, she tried to back up and to make an escape, but he followed and blocked her way.

That did it. 'Take off, will you?' she bit out, between her teeth, incensed at his sexual advance. His face darkened and he shook his head slowly, manoeuvering his body so that she was pinned against the kitchen counter, his body leaning into hers.

'Not this time, darling,' he said softly. 'Not this time. I left you once because you said you wanted me to, but do you know what? I'm beginning to believe you were lying about that. And I'm beginning to wonder just why you did. Underneath all of that spit and fire, you're just a scared little cat, aren't you, Jess? And why is that? Why should just one little kiss frighten the daylights out of you?'

She saw what he was getting to and she couldn't let him make the surmises that would surely follow the questions. He was so dangerously close to the truth, and she couldn't bear it if he knew that she loved him, on top of everything else. It would give him a lever to work with, give him the power to manipulate her.

She let her eyes go cold, mocking, and drifted her gaze slowly up to his face. That slanting, mocking glance made her seem like some exotic witch, her red hair sweeping away off of her forehead and flowing down her neck. 'You, of all people, should know that one little kiss couldn't frighten me away,' she purred, flicking his chin with one finger. 'That is, when I choose to give it. I'm not that big on force, darling. It makes me furious and then I start to throw things, as you well remember.'

'So give it,' he said thickly, watching her lips move with her speech, and her eyes widened at the blatent invitation in his body and voice. She reflected fuzzily, Damien has the sexiest voice I've ever heard, and then she found that she wanted to kiss him as badly as he appeared to want her to.

Why not? What the hell? What difference would one kiss make after all? Throwing caution and good sense to the wind, she found herself smiling provocatively, and she went forward on her toes to place her lips against his, lightly, sensuously moving over them, not attempting to deepen the kiss but just teasing his lips with the sensation of hers flitting back and forth over them. He didn't bend his head to accommodate her, didn't try to touch her with his hands, and she found that she was intensely disappointed, as she let her hands fall away from his neck and she started to fall back.

'Now I'll show you how to really give it,' he muttered, and his hands hauled her hard up against him as his dark head swooped. Her head fell back and her hands instinctively clutched at his shoulders for support and balance, but he was taking no chances and she couldn't have fallen or moved away if she had tried. His mouth punished her as she kept her lips tightly sealed, and she felt a thrill of laughter at his increasingly obvious frustration at his inability to get her to surrender her mouth. His head jerked up and he stared down at her with ebony eyes, breathing harsh and expression forbidding.

'That wasn't how I give it; that was how you take it,' she murmured. 'I was just trying to show you, darling, that it just isn't any good without two active participants.' Their eyes met. Something quivered

between them, and both moved simultaneously to weld
their lips together.

This time there was no holding back from either of
them, the kiss deepening intimately, and she took from
him as much as he took from her. She was vaguely
aware of hands moulding her hips and pulling her hard
against him, and a flood of pure sexual longing
shuddered through her.

Then something hit her and she jerked her mouth
away to say shakily, 'The lady is no longer willing,
Damien. You've had your kiss, now let me go, damn it.'

His face flushed across the hard cheekbones, and his
eyes glittered at her abrupt withdrawal. 'No,' he said
deliberately, forcing her body to stay in intimate
proximity with his own.

With a supreme effort, she tilted her one mobile brow
at him and reminded acidly, 'I don't think you'd like a
repeat of what happened in my apartment the last time
we saw each other. Sure, we click together physically,
but what the hell? You can go to bed with any woman
and still get it on, can't you? What do you do, put a bag
over the poor girl's head, and then it doesn't really
matter who she is anymore? She's just another woman.
Get it through your thick head, if you can. Just a
physical relationship no longer interests me. I was a
fool to settle for so little to begin with. It's just too
boring.'

She watched his mouth thin into a hard, angry line,
saw him struggle inside himself for a brief moment, and
then suddenly he relaxed totally, in a way that made her
stare in bemusement. That wasn't at all like the man she
had known for three years. The Damien she knew
would be just about ready to explode, and would roar
around the house like a furious, caged lion. This
Damien merely smiled at her openly, genuinely, and

bent to place a gentle kiss just by her right ear, saying, 'Well, then, I guess I might as well say goodnight, since it's late. Your father had the right idea in going to bed so early. See you in the morning, Jessie.'

. She stared at the door long after Damien had sauntered through it. Her eyes narrowed. He was playing some kind of game with her, some kind of devious ploy, and was intent on a goal of his own. Now, that sounded more like the Damien she knew (and loved). What was he driving at? What response was he trying to get from her?

Lower lip thrust out in thought, she went slowly into the living room and stared at the few glowing embers still left in the fireplace. Bending, she picked up the poker and shoved at the charred logs. The fire flared up briefly, long enough for her to lay a few more sticks on it and have them catch on fire, and then she backed up, watching the flames absentmindedly. The living room light was still on and she switched it off again, throwing the room once more into that world of red and shadows. It was cosy, private and soothing. She was still so keyed up from the evening's turn of events that she had no desire to go to bed just to toss and turn sleeplessly. She felt like a drink, that's what she felt like. And so she went over to the drinks' cabinet, found her glass still sitting there, and that reminded her of the broken ash tray. She searched the floor and didn't find any glass, so presumed either Damien or her father had picked it up. She shrugged, poured herself a stiff drink, and started back to her favourite chair and then reached back to grab the carafe of brandy. That was settled on the floor by her chair as she settled herself in it, and she stretched out her toes to the flames with a tired sigh.

Why was life such a complicated mess? she asked

herself disgustedly, sipping from her glass from time to time. God only knew. Sometimes she thought that life would be much easier if she were stupid and didn't have the sense to find any problems with herself or her surroundings. But that mood didn't often last long, for she was glad to be the person that she was for the most part, faults included. In fact, she kind of liked herself. Boy, she mused, finishing her glass, it'd sure be nice to have me for a friend. And she poured herself a drink, to toast herself.

If she were to have the last three years back—but no, she knew that, given the choice, she would probably have done the same things with her life. Hindsight may make one see things better, but it didn't necessarily change the situation. She had told Damien the truth when she had said that she was not just dissatisfied with him, but with her whole life, but that wasn't the case three years ago. And she knew that if she had been secure in the knowledge of his love, nothing else would have mattered. She'd too closely intertwined her self with his. Perhaps she was not a very balanced person. Perhaps other people didn't feel quite the way she did, and that was why they were able to go through their lives as placidly as they did. Perhaps she was the only one in the world to put such a desperately important definition on that strange emotional impulse the world called love.

That was a very lonely thought. She finished her glass and poured another. It was something she could definitely drink to.

The terrible part of everything right now was the temptation. There was a devil inside her, whispering to her to break down and marry Damien while she had the chance. What difference did it make, anyway? He could give to her just as much as he would be able to give to anyone else. Why shouldn't she be the one to take what he offered and hope that he may learn to love her back, just a little?

But that was the kind of rationalisation that she had gone through three years ago, and she was no longer the same person. She was older, no longer full of that eager optimism, and she was tired. She envisioned hell as being the kind of existence that marriage with Damien would bring her. Living with someone you love and realising that he didn't love you back, now that was hell. She toasted hell and then toasted temptation.

She rather thought she was getting good and drunk after a while, because the carafe was beginning to empty. That was strange, because she had been tipsy once or twice before but never drunk, and she had thought that when one was drunk, one tended to do crazy things. She toasted craziness, and then she toasted drunkenness, and then she toasted her toes, because there were four feet at the end of her legs and that certainly deserved a good drink.

One pair of toes gradually went away, and she drank to that, hiccuping slightly and snickering to herself. Life wasn't so bad. All you needed was the right perspective on things. She lifted her glass to silently toast perspectivity and then frowned owlishly at the fire. Was perspectivity a word?

She tried it out loud and found that her tongue was not doing quite what it was told to do. 'Perseckity. Perstickiby. Persnickity.' That last one made her giggle insanely. If it hadn't already been a word, she would have invented a new one. She tried again, 'Sperpeckity,' and snorted hilariously at that one because that had been the weirdest of all. She solemnly toasted sperpeckity—and was at the end of her glass.

A quiet, resigned voice said beside her, 'Don't you think you've had enough, darling?'

She turned her head so fast she had to take a minute to focus her eyes on Damien. He had on a pair of tight jeans and that was all, with bare chest showing a light sprinkle of hairs, and bare feet. His black hair was tousled and his face seemed to be tired, but his eyes were alert and patiently humorous.

'I don't know,' she said clearly, and then spoiled it all by snickering behind one hand. Her eyes reflected the gold from the fire, and they twinkled merrily up at him, and if they were still slightly unfocused, he had the tact not to mention it.

He squatted down and fished around for the carafe, and found it almost empty. 'Good Lord! You've managed to pack away a hellish amount of brandy. I hate to tell you this, darling, but you are going to have one terrible hangover in the morning. You should know better than that at your age.'

'What does age have t'do with anything?' she asked, indignantly, bristling at his reference to her age. 'I knew what I was drinking, din't I? S'all relative, time and age, anyhows. Everybody's relative. I think I'll call you Uncle Damie.'

He laughed at that, shaking his head at her, white smile slashing across his face. 'I was on my way to the bathroom and realised that your door was open, so I thought I'd stick my head in the door and check on you since you had sworn to me you were going to lock your door and sure enough! You're never where you are supposed to be, my girl. So I come down here and what do I find? You mumbling under your breath and giggling like a lunatic! Did you have to go and get stinking drunk?'

'Skunk as a drunk, tha's what I thunk,' she said wisely, and pealed off again into a fit of laughter. She regarded him owlishly, contemplatively. He had one arm propped on the arm rest of her chair, so he was very near, and firelight rippled on his bare skin, turning his chest a warm, golden brown. She loved to look at his body. He had a warmth and an essence of strength that she craved. She looked down at his thick forearm and put her fingers on it to run them across four evenly spaced burn scars, obviously old and interrupting the pattern of hair. He would never talk about them, just answering indifferently that he had an accident as a child, and she had never felt comfortable enough to press the issue. They were as familiar to her as the rest of his body was, and her fingers traced them each. 'Did I ever tell you, Uncle Damie, tha' you haf a nice body? A'ways thought so. A'ways thought you did. Nice guy, you know it? Yer a nice body, but tha's insect, Uncle Damie.' At that she buried her head helplessly in her hands and shook with laughter.

Soft chuckles answered her and Damien slid his arms gently around her to try and lift her up. 'I think it's well past this little girl's bedtime. Come on, I'll get you up the stairs.'

'Stop it, stop it!' she argued loudly, slapping at him and trying to push his arms away. 'I kin dew it. I'll walk it myseff.' And with that she tried to stand and the world swayed so that she had to grab hold of his arm. He tried to put it around her but she pushed herself away from him and tried a few experimental steps. 'Whoops! Could you pick up the bottle for me, Uncle Damie? I don' think I'd better bend down. Hey, look, I ain't walkin' so bad, am I?'

She turned carefully and promptly ran into a wall, and just leaned her head against it, giggling uproariously. 'S'all a matter of—of specta-persivy. Persativity. Ah, hell. Damien, the wall moved.'

'Will you just let me pick you up?' he asked her resignedly, still laughing at the comical sight she produced. She nodded and moaned as the world did a strange dance all around her, and her body started to slide sideways as she leaned against the wall. He caught her and slowly lifted her up so that she wouldn't be too disoriented by the motion.

Jessica let her head fall on to his bare shoulder with a sigh of relief. 'Couldn't miss the side of a barn,' she confessed cheerfully, and his shoulder muscle flexed beneath her cheek.

'I know it. You'd probably walk smack into it at the rate you're going,' he whispered. 'Now, be quiet. We don't want to wake your father.'

She nodded solemnly, and pressed her cheek closer to his shoulder. He was holding her so carefully, as if he really cared about her, and he felt so good. She thought that his head came down on top of hers for a moment but felt so fuzzy she couldn't be sure. She gave in to temptation and turned her mouth to press it against his skin, letting her tongue touch him, tasting him. 'Mmn, delicious,' she murmured. 'You taste better than any ol' brandy, Damien.'

She felt his whole body stiffen and heard the harsh intake of his breath. Then laughter shook his chest and voice as he deposited her on her own bed after pulling back the covers. 'Lord, lady, you sure pick your times. No, don't unbutton my jeans! You can taste me some other time if you still feel like it, I promise! Now, help me get you out of your clothes.'

'Why?' she asked suspiciously, trying to peer at him through the darkness. She felt so tired.

'Because you'll feel more comfortable without them, that's why.'

'Oh,' she said, digesting this. She shrugged. 'Okay.'

With some difficulty, he managed to get her under the covers in spite of her help, and he tucked the sheet up under her chin with a gentle kiss to her up-turned nose. She sighed at that and snuggled right down like a small child, except for the smell of liquor.

'Oh, darling,' he sighed, 'you really reek.'

'Oh?' she said curiously, opening one eye again to try and find him, but all she saw was darkness and her eye fluttered shut. 'Wreak what, havoc? S'all perspeckibility, Uncle Damie. G'night.'

CHAPTER EIGHT

WHEN Jessica finally opened her eyes the next morning, she closed them again quickly, groaning in pain. The groan had been a mistake also, she found, for it seemed to reverberate through the corridors of her mind, twanging at sore nerve endings and making her head pound achingly. A hangover! She had a stupid hangover, for heaven's sake, and she had never had one before in her life. Her eyelids felt swollen and her tongue stuck to the roof of her dry mouth. She had to get a drink of water before she died of thirst.

Sitting as gingerly as possible, she moaned again as the room danced crazily around and around. The motion was getting to be too much. A wave of nausea so acute and overwhelming had her shooting out of bed and running for the bathroom at full speed.

Some time later, shuddering in the aftermath of the bout of stomach sickness, Jessica searched through the medicine cabinet for some bicarbonate of soda for her still queasy stomach, and aspirin for her poor, pounding head. She mixed up the soda and sipped at it carefully, but her stomach was much too sensitive and it all came right back up again.

Eventually she managed to get dressed and then she crept down the stairs, hanging grimly on to the banister, since the steps seemed to be moving around of their own volition. It was very late, she saw, as she inched carefully past the clock in the living room, and she began to wonder where her father and Damien were. In the kitchen she went slowly about the motions of making coffee, and that too was a mistake, for as soon as the pungent aroma wafted to her quivering nostrils, her stomach again revolted, and this time the sickness was much more painful since she no longer had anything in her stomach to come up.

Uncertain as to what she should clutch at, either her abdomen or her head, she instead reluctantly made her way back to the kitchen so she could turn off the brewer in the coffeemaker before the machine was ruined, and she found that she could stand the smell of the coffee now, though just barely. That surely must be a good sign, she thought, and she poured herself a cup with an unsteady hand. Then she went back upstairs and got the bicarbonate of soda so that she could mix herself another dose. She couldn't bolster up enough courage to try either drink, having no desire to prompt another bout of nausea, and so when Will and Damien entered the kitchen some minutes later, they found her with her head lying on her folded arms, sitting at the kitchen table with both untouched drinks in front of her.

Will shut the back door behind him and she jerked in her chair. 'Oh, my God!' she moaned achingly, covering her ears. 'You're going to kill me with all of that racket! Couldn't you at least try to be a little more quiet?'

The two men looked at each other over Jessica's bright, bent head, Will's eyebrows shooting up and Damien's well-formed lips beginning to tremble at the corners.

'Your father merely pushed the door closed,' Damien said mildly, his face threatening to split into laughter. 'He didn't even slam it. What's the matter, Jess? Is your head hurting a little this morning?'

She turned her face towards them and opened one baleful eye. Her face was very pale and there were circles under her eyes, dark bruised shadows that made her face look very fragile. 'If you don't stop screaming at me at the top of your lungs, I may get violent.'

A chuckle burst forth from Damien and she scowled at his crass insensitivity, while her father remarked, 'I think I'm beginning to understand why you thought we should just let her sleep in this morning instead of inviting her to go with us. Whatever happened, or need I ask?'

'Do you know what your daughter got into?' Damien said, his voice quivering slightly. 'She just about finished off that carafe of very excellent brandy you had in the liquor cabinet, Will.'

'Oh my! That entire carafe?' His eyebrows shot up even more than before, and he started to smile. 'No wonder you're feeling ... ah, a bit under the weather. Well, that too will pass, my dear, no matter how you feel differently at the moment. I must say, I shall miss that brandy.'

'I'll get you more,' Damien promised. 'But I think you may have to hide it from Jessica if she's going to turn into a regular little lush.'

'Ha,' she muttered, without any particular emphasis. She really wished that they would stop talking and go away, so that she could recover in relative peace and quiet. She felt so fragile, she was afraid that she was going to break into a thousand little pieces at any undue sound.

She had closed her eyes again, and so when she heard some movement about the kitchen, she didn't know what to expect until a distinct fishy odour assailed her too sensitive nose, and her father was saying, 'Well, I guess I'd better start to clean up the fish if we're going to have them for lunch.'

'Oh, no,' she moaned sickly, turning a peculiar shade

of green and clutching at her stomach. A strange churning feeling came over her and she bolted from her seat like a bat out of hell. Damien was already ahead of her, holding the swinging door open as she shot out into the hall and ran up the stairs. She made it to the bathroom and shoved the door shut behind her and then she was wrenchingly, violently sick. Shudder after shudder wracked her body painfully, and she was too wrapped up in her nausea to even care when two cool supporting hands came around her neck and chin to help her through the painful convulsions. She was grateful for the support for she was beginning to feel weak after so much sickness. Afterwards, however, as she sat on the tiled floor in the bathroom and leaned against the side of the bathrub, she became acutely self-conscious and said snappily, 'Will you just get out of here and let a person die in peace?'

Damien had stood and was running some cold water over a flannel, and he then bent to press the cool cloth to her hot forehead with gentle fingers. He said sympathetically, 'Hangovers are hellish, aren't they? But I promise you, darling, that you aren't going to die. You may wish yourself dead before you feel better, but you won't expire from too much brandy one night. I know, I've been there.'

'If I was just left alone, I might, just might, recover,' she muttered pettishly, and then sighed as the cloth eased away some of the discomfort. She turned her face to it and to his gentle hands, and he continued to wipe rhythmically across her forehead and cheeks and neck. 'That feels marvellous.'

'Mmn,' he responded automatically, and then he said, strangely, 'Do you know, this is the first time I think I've ever seen you sick? How very odd. I never noticed it before. You must be very healthy.'

'I must look like a monster,' she groaned, remembering and turning her face away from him in an effort to hide. 'I'm usually not sick, but when I was you were always away on business trips.'

He held still at that and the silence stretched out before he slid closer so that he could continue to administer to her face and neck. 'I am very sorry about that, and I know it sounds terribly inadequate, but it's the only thing I have to say,' he said quietly. 'You don't look like a monster, so stop squirming around and let me get at you! You're just a bit pink around the eyes, maybe, and very pale, but other than that you are just as beautiful as ever. How you can manage to look so good after a night of the kind of drinking you indulged in last night is beyond my powers of comprehension. Do you feel ill anymore?'

She considered that with her head leaning against his shoulder. It was so nice, just to let go and lean on someone else, so nice not to feel that she had to be strong no matter what, so nice to have Damien's arms around her. 'No, I don't think so. I was really feeling a little better until I caught a whiff of that fish!' She shivered at the memory. 'Ugh! I'll never be able to look a main dish of fish in the face again!'

'Now, it's not as bad as all that,' he soothed, sliding his other arm beneath her and flexing his shoulder muscles as he stood, picking her up. 'I think you'd feel better in bed for a while longer. I can bring your drinks up for you and you can go to sleep after finishing them. How does that sound?'

Jessica had a brief struggle between her pride and her inclinations, and her inclinations won out. 'That sounds good,' she sighed. 'Maybe I can get rid of this headache then.' She gave herself up totally to the sensation of relaxing and letting someone else take care of her for a change, as Damien strode out into the landing and into her bedroom. He hesitated for a minute as he looked from the unmade bed to her face, and she said quickly, 'It'd be too much trouble to undress again. Just let me pull up the covers and then I'll lie down on top of them.' Her head was pounding vilely and all she wanted to do was to collapse in a heap somewhere, with as little fuss as possible.

He read the expression on her face, nodded, and set her on her feet for a moment to yank the covers up again. He was barely done before she was sliding on to the bed like a wet noodle slipping on to an empty plate, and she settled right where she landed, closing her eyes with something like desperation. She missed his regard and slight smile and shake of his head, but she did feel something pass over her hair, like a quick caress. Then his footsteps sounded out the door.

He was back quickly enough, with both the glass of soda and the cup of coffee, and he sat carefully down on the edge of her bed with both. 'Which would you like first?'

She opened one red-rimmed eye. 'You can have the coffee, thanks. I'm not going to press my luck.' She took the proffered glass and began to sip at it carefully, making an involuntary grimace of distaste as the liquid went down. 'If I survive this, it'll be a miracle, nothing less.' She peered at him with her one eye. He was sitting, sipping at the hot brew in the cup, his dark head bent over it and his eyes thoughtfully fixed on something on the opposite wall. She loved to look at him, loved to run her eyes down the lines of his body, the angle of his strong neck, the implication of power in the width and bulge of his shoulder muscles, the sleek hips. Even sick as she was, she could appreciate the inherent sensuality in him.

He turned his head quickly and smiled at the one eye peeping at him. She had finished her drink and was snuggling down into her pillow. 'Tell me something?' he asked softly, and the other eye emerged to regard him warily.

'I wish this room would quit spinning,' she complained mildly. 'Maybe I will and maybe I won't. It depends on what you want to know.' She didn't trust those black, merry eyes. They sobered quickly, though, as he asked his question.

'Why did you get drunk last night, Jess? What were you trying to cope with?'

'Sorry,' she muttered, flushing slightly, 'privileged information.' She remembered how she had struggled with her feelings and longings last night, and she could never tell him of that, not in a million years. Her eyes fell away from his gaze and she shrugged, an infinitesimal, uncertain movement. 'I guess things just got to me, that's all.'

She tensed as his hand came to stroke her cheek down to her slim neck, and she turned her face away, inadvertently giving him an excellent view of the slender bones in her jaw and neck, and the abrupt shock of the red scar along what was otherwise a perfect profile. 'What things?' he whispered persuasively, but she shook her head. He finally said, 'Okay, not now, then. You get some sleep.'

Her voice came back softly. 'Not ever, Damien. Some things should be left private.'

A weary sigh answered her and she turned her head back as he said strangely, tiredly, 'I, too, used to think that.' That made her go very still until he broke the spell with a slightly unsteady laugh. 'You look very cosy all curled up like that. I just may join you.'

She groaned out an involuntary chuckle. 'Not now,

Damien, please! I have a headache.' And she watched his eyes light up with amusement before she rolled over to fall asleep.

When she woke up the day had slipped away into the late afternoon. This was a slight jar to her senses, for she was the type of person to be up early in the morning, eager to get things done. As she got out of bed, feeling almost normal again, she wondered briefly if Damien had decided to go back to New York or not. With this in mind, she took the stairs two at a time, pulling up short at the bottom as she took in the sight of Damien slouched in her favourite easy chair, feet stretched towards a cheery fire, reading a book.

'Well,' she drawled, eyeing him askance as she strolled over to stand near the fire. 'This is certainly something new. You never had the time to read at home.'

He was smiling even before he looked up, and he was quick to lay the book aside. 'Welcome back to the land of the living, darling. I guess I'd forgotten how relaxing and enjoyable a good book can be. This could be cultivated into a habit, I think.'

She reached down and picked up the book, looking at the title with astonishment. 'He's even reading fiction, and a chilling mystery at that! Wonders never cease, after all. You must have gotten this out of my father's library. He eats these kind of books for breakfast.'

'Yes, it's a loan for the duration of my stay.'

At that her head snapped around and her eyes narrowed warily. 'Staying, then?' she questioned cautiously. 'Just exactly how long do you intend to stay?'

'Didn't I tell you?' he replied innocently, his head tilted back to survey her expression better. 'I've decided to take your father up on his offer and am staying at least for another three days, possibly a week.'

Her pupils widened, and she had to swallow once before she could get anything out of her throat. It wasn't that she was surprised; she'd expected something like this. She was, however, extremely discomfited at the thought of him being in such close proximity to her for any length of time. 'Maybe I'd better sit down for a minute,' she said conversationally, groping for a chair behind her. She sank into it and regarded Damien's outwardly placid exterior thoughtfully. He seemed fully relaxed, with long legs kicked out in front of him and arms draped on the arm rests, lean fingers linked loosely together. To almost anyone he would appear to be totally at his ease, indolent even, but Jessica was narrowing knowledgeable eyes on him and realised that he was about as relaxed as a wildcat about to spring. 'I don't believe that I've ever known you to take even an entire weekend off, let alone a full seven days. Are you sure that your business will survive without you for that long?' That last was said with a touch of malice.

His chin sank to his chest and he looked at her from under lowered, considering brows for a moment, as if deciding what to say. 'I'd taken the time to arrange things before I came up here,' he replied, with every appearance of tranquillity, except that his eyes glittered watchfully. And she saw it. 'Otherwise I might have been here sooner.'

She was nodding even before he had finished speaking. Damien had not just intended a flying visit, just to ask her to marry him and then graciously accept a refusal. He had come with every intention of doing everything in his power to get her acceptance. He really had his mind set this time.

'I think I begin to get the picture,' she said calmly. 'It

does take me a while sometimes, but I'm not totally moronic or senile. Excuse me.' She rose and headed for the kitchen and heard behind her the immediate creaking of the chair and footsteps following hers.

'Now, just a minute, Jessica,' he said impatiently, and she turned slowly to face him, her left eyebrow cocked warningly and mouth pursed.

'Make it quick, will you?' she said snappily. 'I'm so hungry I think my stomach is eating through my backbone.'

He stopped and stared at her with the beginnings of puzzlement in his eyes. 'You were going to the kitchen?'

'Of course.' She swung around and continued on down the hall, throwing over her shoulder, 'Where did you think I was going?'

'I thought you were going to go upstairs to pack your things,' he admitted quietly, coming into the kitchen with her. He watched her peruse the contents of the refrigerator. She could feel his gaze like a physical touch, and she concentrated on keeping her face completely blank. 'I'll make us coffee if you'd like some.'

'Okay.' Underneath her uncaring exterior, Jessica was doing some rapid thinking of her own. The only reason that she had come to the kitchen in the first place instead of going to pack was because she was starving, and before Damien had come right out and said it, she'd had every intention of going upstairs and getting her clothes together and to run away if she absolutely had to. Now she saw that it wouldn't work, and she wasn't going to give Damien the satisfaction or the knowledge that he had upset her so much that she had felt she had to retreat again. She was going to show him that it didn't matter to her one way or the other if he stayed, because as far as she was concerned their relationship had been finished in New York. She was going to put on a first-class act.

She knew that he was looking at her from time to time, studying her face reflectively, assessingly. And she suddenly had a quiver of uncertainty as to whether she could pull off the act or not, because he did frighten her and threaten her, and his very presence put all of her newfound serenity and resolve in severe jeopardy. She was actually going to try to deceive one of the keenest intellectual minds in the country? Part of his tremendous success in his business was his ability to judge people and assess their sincerity and honesty. He probably dealt with people like her all of the time. Well, she thought, mentally squaring her shoulders, it was all a matter of relativity, anyway, because she had years of experience of being in front of an impartial, inhuman camera eye that picked up every line of stress and nuance of expression that was let past her control. And one had to exercise an iron control for that kind of exposure. She found herself smoothly clicking into the role of a social hostess, as if some master mechanism had pulled a lever in her mind. She suddenly found that she could trust her own ability to act after all; it would be her expertise in hiding her true feelings pitted against his ability to see past them.

'Did you want a snack also? I don't know what to have,' she chatted conversationally, ticking off the items in the refrigerator with one forefinger. 'I'm so hungry and yet I'm afraid that if I eat anything too spicy, it might all come right back up again. How long will it take before my stomach is back to normal, do you think?'

'I think this is going to be harder than I had first anticipated,' he told the coffeemaker, and then peered over his shoulder at her. 'You should be feeling quite well by tomorrow, no doubt. If you'd like, I'll fix us an omelette, or there's soup. Fish doesn't sound very good to you?'

She shuddered delicately and moved away, shutting the refrigerator door with a quick casual shove. 'No, thank you! I guess I'll just have coffee, please.'

At that, he frowned heavily. 'You haven't had anything to eat for almost twenty-four hours. You'll really make yourself sick, if you don't eat. Come on,' he coaxed. 'How about if I fix you a nice light salad?'

She shrugged indifferently and he chose to take that as an affirmative. Pushing her into a chair and pouring her a cup of coffee, he told her kindly to shut up and be good while he went about the process of fixing her something to eat. At first she really was indifferent to his preparations, but as she sipped the coffee and it hit her empty stomach, she began to feel hungrier and hungrier. When he finally set the light snack in front of her, she was more than ready to fall on it with a delicate pounce, which caused him to smile. He sat and watched her eat.

'Feel better?'

She glanced up and found him looking at her tolerantly. 'Oh, yes!' she replied, mouth full. 'This is really hitting the spot, thank you.'

'You're quite welcome.' He leaned back, sipped at his coffee, and continued easily, 'I can remember when fresh produce like lettuce was a rare luxury for us. We were lucky if we got enough to fill our stomachs, let alone any of what we called the "extras".'

Her eyes swung up to his swiftly. He was actually making the effort to talk about his past again. She blinked, feeling less astonishment than she might have in the past. Anything seemed possible with this new Damien, anything at all. And this, she privately admitted, was partly what frightened her about him. He no longer fitted into the niche that she had erected for him. He had burst out of the mould her conception of him had created, and he was an unknown force to be reckoned with.

'I'll bet that your mother had to work hard just to make ends meet,' she murmured sympathetically, and had to gulp when his expression unexpectedly darkened into something like fury.

'Work!' he exclaimed shortly, sourly, and the bitterness so apparent in his voice made her wince. 'I guess that's one euphemism for what she did. No, Jessica, I don't think my mother worked an honest day in her life. I can't even begin to count the "uncles" we all had. Some of them stayed a few days, some a few weeks. A few came after we were supposed to be asleep and were gone by morning. Do you know what her favourite pastime was? She used to spend her afternoons in the local bar, trying to get anyone she could to buy her drinks. That's where she met most of her men friends. She lived pretty decently on what her boyfriends gave her, and we got the leftovers. God, I almost feel sorry for the man who had married her and took off one day, the poor bastard. It's no wonder, is it?'

Her face had whitened at Damien's succinct wording, shocked more than she wanted to admit at this glimpse of his past. 'Oh, Damien,' she whispered, impulsively reaching out to grasp at his knuckled fist that rested on the table. 'I had no idea——'

His hand moved, turned under hers and gripped her hand tightly. 'How could you?' he asked, the strange bitter look fading from his eyes and being replaced by something more mocking. This shocked her also, until she realised that he was mocking himself, not her.

'When I never tried to tell you any of it? I spent all my life in fear that my past was going to crop up and confront me and that I wasn't going to be able to handle it, and all of the time it was me who kept it alive and let it cripple me. You know, for someone who's supposed to be intelligent, I have certainly been a fool. What did you ever see in me?'

She had to laugh and then sobered suddenly when she considered the question seriously. 'I don't know anymore. I can't seem to look back and get a clear picture of how I viewed you. I guess it's because my comprehension of you has been so drastically changed and broadened lately. We seem to be undergoing some kind of metamorphosis, some kind of personality change, I——'

'No,' he interrupted gently, squeezing her hand so tightly that she winced from the pressure. 'It's no personality change, Jess. We're just growing into the people that for a long time we wouldn't let ourselves be. In a way we were quite a bit like your Mary Mouse, refusing to change into what we could be for fear of losing what we had.'

'I didn't treat you right, all those years!' she burst out, feeling guilt-ridden at how she had subtly deceived him. The burden, the curse, and possibly the salvation of mankind must be guilt and one's conscience, she thought, agonised. God help us all. 'I'm so very sorry, Damien!'

'Oh, Lord,' he groaned, 'Jess, you don't have anything to be sorry for! I'm the one who should be down on my knees, begging your forgiveness.'

'Please,' she whispered, touching his lips with one feather-light finger. 'Let me be truthful with you, for once. For probably the first time since I've known you. Sometimes I feel so ashamed because you've never tried to be anything but truthful with me and it's the one gift you freely gave. It was a hard gift at times, but it was real. Don't look so agonized! I just want to tell you how sorry I am, for not treating you as if you were a real human being. I put you on a pedestal, raised you and my own expectations too high! You were the tall, dark and handsome stranger in my life, the knight who would if given enough time right all of the wrongs around me and take away all of the loneliness and the pain, and anything that happened to be unsatisfactory in my life. No one should be expected to handle that kind of burden, and even though you may not have consciously realised what I was doing, you must have known. You went away when the pressure became too much, when it became too obvious that I was expecting you to make some kind of commitment you weren't prepared to make, and I can't tell you how sorry I am.'

'Jessie, don't,' he said, his expression tightening, becoming pained. 'Don't do this to yourself. You don't deserve it. I was the one at fault for not recognising your needs.'

Weak tears filled her eyes and she passed a hand over her face quickly, blinking the moisture away and avoiding Damien's steady, pain-filled gaze. 'Is this really necessary?' she asked chokily, struggling to get herself in hand. 'Do we really need to go through all of this?'

'I think so,' was his quiet reply, forcing her to glance back at him by the sheer compulsion of his intense gaze. 'Yes, I think so, if we are to learn from the past, heal ourselves and go on. Isn't that what you tried to tell me yesterday? I think you were right.'

She looked at her hands in her lap and tried to smile. It was a dismal attempt. 'To put it behind us.'

'No. To take a part of it with us.' He reached out a

sudden, gentle finger and traced the outline of her smooth jaw. It was such a clean, pure line, beautifully in proportion with the rest of her profile, and he stroked it as if he really loved the look and feel of her. This isn't fair, she thought, closing her eyes and starting to tremble. He's caught me when my resistance is low. I can't keep resisting him.

Moving violently, Jessica brought both of her hands down flat on the table, shoved hard, and as her chair scooted on the tiled kitchen floor, she came up and was out of the room before her chair had stopped moving. She strode for the front door with long purposeful strides, because she knew that if she didn't get out of the house and away from Damien now, she would soon lose all of her strength of mind.

Jessica knew what hell was. She'd thought last night that hell would be to marry Damien while knowing that he didn't love her. That wasn't hell. Hell was just being near him and knowing he didn't love her. She impatiently shook her head at the pain. She was tired of feeling pain and enduring a situation that was unendurable. She couldn't believe that she'd actually put up with that kind of hell for three years. She was not very proud of herself.

'Jessica!' Damien rapped out, and she heard rapid footsteps behind her. 'Where are you going? What's the matter with you? Is something wrong?'

She stopped just inside the front door and turned to face him angrily. She felt pushed to the limit, felt that band of control on her emotions being pulled taut to the breaking point. The frustration showed in her eyes and compressed mouth and the clenching and unclenching of her hands.

'I am going out,' she said, between her teeth and staring at him as if she hated him. The upper half of his body was in shadow and she couldn't see his face, but his body was held absolutely still, quiet. 'And you are not invited. No, I don't know what time I'll be back, and wouldn't tell you if I did. I don't care what you think or want, and I frankly don't care if you get angry at me and leave, but this is *my* vacation and you are trespassing on my time. Now for the first time in several days, I'm going to get out and enjoy myself.'

And he didn't say anything as she turned and stormed out the door. And what could he say? she asked silently. Nothing. Everything was said and the post mortem was complete. She would avoid him until he chose to leave, and then she would say a polite goodbye and heave a sigh of relief as he walked out the door. Would she? Would she? She moaned, desperately, and started to walk briskly down the street, anxious to get as much space between her and Damien as she could.

But she couldn't run away from her own chaotic, tortured thoughts.

The shadows were lengthening into black murky pools of ink when she finally turned into the sidewalk that led up to the house. She was tired and hungry and emotionally drained, and the last thing she wanted to do now was to face Damien again. She had put off coming back, walking block after block until her feet ached and her side was shot through with a white hot pain. It couldn't be done, she couldn't run away. She'd tried it once and it didn't work. It wasn't worth trying again, but oh, how she wanted to.

Grasping the doorknob with a slightly shaking hand, she stepped into the house and stared at the two men who had slewed around in their seats at her entrance. Will's gaze was concerned, questioning, and Damien's dark eyes held some kind of leaping emotion that she didn't even attempt to understand. She looked at them for a moment, her jaw set, and then headed for the kitchen without a word.

As she filled up a kettle for some hot tea, Damien said from the doorway, 'There's some supper in the oven, if you're hungry.'

Still silent, she set the kettle down and turned on the heat, and then took the oven gloves and removed the leftover casserole from the oven and started to dish it on to a plate. There was no sound from the doorway, and she wanted badly to know if Damien was still there or not, but wouldn't turn around to look. She couldn't relax, and her shoulder muscles bunched painfully into knots of tension. This was going to make her sick if something didn't change pretty soon. She couldn't take it for much longer.

'Jessica.' His voice was very quiet. 'Are you all right?'

Silence. She banged her plate down on to the counter and heard the protesting clank! Then she reached up and grabbed at a coffee cup. She didn't want to trust herself to speak at the moment. She wasn't sure if she could control herself.

'Jess?' A thread of impatience, this time. 'Are you even going to answer me?'

She turned abruptly, stared at him with hard bright eyes. 'Get out. I don't want to talk to you, get out.' Something must have convinced him to leave, something about her rigid stance, the lines of tiredness on her face, the violent quality to her words. He looked at her for a moment under frowning brows and then quietly left the room.

She slumped, and found that she hadn't wanted him to leave after all. And that self-knowledge made her want to cry.

It was a solitary, silent meal. Afterwards, she went

into the living room, without a look either right or left, and picked up her book that she'd left by her chair. Then she marched up to her room, slammed and locked the door. And she studiously avoided any contact with Damien.

The next morning she ate her breakfast alone, pushed by him silently in the hall, and busied herself with mundane, household chores. She saw the warning signals well enough. She saw his countenance darken after a while, and his jaw tighten dangerously. She knew that he would not put up with such rudeness for long, and the knowledge gave her an angry satisfaction. She wanted to goad him into losing his temper. She wanted to see him flare up, like he could make her flare up. She wanted a good knock-down, drag-out fight, for there was an answering anger and tension in her just aching to be released.

The confrontation came, but in a way that she had least expected.

Her father had gone to the shop some time ago, and she had assumed that Damien was out, for the silence in the house felt empty and complete, and had been silent for at least half an hour. She sighed heavily, shoulders drooping as she absently dusted the small table that sat near one of the easy chairs. She had been dusting the same table for some time now and had never realised it, as thoughts chased each other around and around. Why was Damien staying? How much more of this silent battle could either of them take? When would it end? She was tired of the questions, for the same ones kept echoing in her head, unanswered.

A noise behind her made her whirl around apprehensively, and he was there, just standing in the middle of the room, sunlight reflecting off his black hair and bouncing off hard angles in his set face. He didn't say anything but just stood there, staring at her, and finally she couldn't take that brooding scrutiny any longer. She stood up jerkily, threw down her duster, and headed out the room, right past him, face averted and heart thumping madly. He wasn't going to put up with it, she thought, he wasn't going to sit back and take this. And she was profoundly surprised as she was able to walk right by him and climb up the stairs, uninterrupted.

Her relief came too soon. As she reached the top of the stairs and headed down the hall to her bedroom, a slight noise sent her heart racing madly again. She risked a glance behind her and then turned around fully as she saw Damien following her closely with that same, set expression on his face. It was beginning to frighten her. She stopped. 'Now, look——' she started firmly, and then suddenly stopped and gasped as he grasped hold of her upper arm and shoved her forcibly into her own room. Pushed into the middle of the floor, she turned and was about to snap irritably at him, and her eyes widened as he stopped and carefully locked the door. Then he leaned against it, arms crossed purposefully, and his steady and determined gaze unnerved her more than anything else.

'Now, then,' he said calmly. 'This is it. You aren't going to run any more, Jessica. I've had it.'

CHAPTER NINE

SHE hissed furiously, 'Get out of my room, dammit!' He came away from the door and started to leisurely walk across the room, his dark gaze never leaving her face. She swallowed, and then quietly began to back up, herself.

'Perhaps you didn't hear what I just said,' he continued pleasantly, and she didn't like that pleasant voice, not one bit. Damien being pleasant with that smouldering fire in his eyes was not the kind of confrontation she had had in mind. 'I'll repeat myself, then. I've had it. I've had all I'm going to take of your rudeness and your sidestepping the issue. I'm tired of this. Sit down.'

And Jessica found herself sitting, as he reached out a sudden, swift hand and pushed her into the seat by the window. He came close, and then knelt beside her, putting both arms on the two arm rests and then leaning far too close to her for comfort.

Her reaction to this was maddening to her, for her heart was racing much too fast and her lips were suddenly and inexplicably dry, and she found her hands shaking so violently that she clasped them together in her lap and twisted her fingers together. This apprehension was not what she had envisioned when she had realised that she was goading Damien beyond what was really safe. And she started to get angry at him. She didn't like being pushed into chairs and locked into rooms, and she especially didn't like feeling as threatened as she did.

But what he said next deflated her so much that all she could do was sag in her seat and look at him blankly.

'I'm on my knees,' he said quietly, flatly, just looking at her with those dark, violent, leaping eyes. She stared. 'I'll beg, if that's what you want, if that will convince you that I'm totally serious. I need you. I need your warmth and beauty, your laughter and your tears. That's why I kept coming back to see you—I couldn't stay away. Don't walk away from me, Jess. Don't walk away now. The other—I can't say the other just yet, but for now, I'm admitting something I've never said to another human being. Jessica, I need you.'

Feeling incredibly moved and close to tears, she let her gaze fall to the open collar of his shirt. The column of his throat rose with such a corded strength from masculinely graceful collarbones. She so loved the beauty of him. And she had to close her eyes as a wave of love and longing swept over her and rocked the foundation of her resolve and all her intentions. It was all there, wrapped in as nice a package as she would ever get. Damien was making huge strides in admitting that he needed her—surely that would be enough for anyone. Need was akin to love, and that would hopefully come in time. He had begun to put the past behind him, and that too was a huge stride in the right direction. She rather suspected that his deep mistrust of relationships and women came from his mother's conduct in his early years. How could he help but feel such a deep wariness and reluctance to commit himself to more possible pain? She found it incredible that he had managed to achieve so much when lesser personalities were so often crippled for life from their past. And she sensed with a deep inner certainty that this was it, her very last chance, the final offer. He wouldn't ask again. He had just got on his knees for her; if she rejected him now, she knew that Damien would never ask again.

She said shakily, 'I'm so afraid. I don't want to ask any more than you can give, I don't want to make too many demands on you. You need someone who is good around the house, someone willing to stay home and take care of you, and I'm not cut out for that kind of life. I couldn't just be a wife, I'd have to have something to occupy myself with, something to challenge me——'

His eyebrows had shot up at her words, and he interrupted gently, 'I don't want you to change for me. I'm asking you to come to me just the way you are. I have a housekeeper, why would I want to marry one? You should be what you're meant to be, and that's the part I value most about you. I think you're making obstacles that don't really exist.'

'But my terrible temper,' she protested. It was a weak sound, and they both knew it.

'Can you think of anyone better than I who could handle that? We're alike, you and I, because we feel things deeply, personally, and our anger goes deep. And, I can afford just about anything you smash up,' he said humorously, with a gentle malice that reminded her of her outburst in her apartment.

She was giving in, she could feel herself giving in inside, and knew that her struggle was lost the moment she looked into his steady, compelling gaze. She was floundering and she didn't want to save herself—until something occurred to her. Her gaze focused sharply, and she said suddenly, 'Promise me something. The rest—it doesn't matter if you don't want to give it, but if you don't promise me one thing it won't work, and I won't even try.'

'Anything.' It was said without hesitation.

Shaken, she whispered, 'You're that sure?' and he nodded, unsmiling. She took a deep breath, nostrils flaring tensely, wondering how to say what she wanted to say. Then she expelled her breath gustily, knowing there was no point in being anything but succinct. 'I want your fidelity. I'm just not by nature able to handle any other kind of marriage, and——'

'You wonderful little simpleton, I haven't been with another woman for over two years,' he said simply. 'Do you mean to tell me that you really couldn't tell?'

She felt stunned at this more than anything else. 'All of those months of meaningless jealousy,' she whispered. 'And I never realised—my God, I never realised!' She could see how obvious it really was, now that she was not obsessed with her insecurities and jealousy. Whenever he had come back to her after weeks or months away, their lovemaking had had a kind of starving ferocity, a quality of intensity that should have told her more than anything else. She didn't have to search any further than her memory; she believed him.

'Does this mean,' Damien was asking carefully, his eyes averted, 'that you are going to consider marriage, without throwing out the idea right away?'

'I'm a fool, but I'm going to say yes, anyway,' she replied quietly, and she saw him close his eyes and swallow hard, as if he were immensely relieved, and then he was wrapping his arms around her and dragging her close to kiss her in that fierce, starving way she remembered so well. It sparked off a similar kind of response in her as all of the cold and lonely nights suddenly accumulated into a need that she could no longer suppress. She wound her arms tremblingly around his waist, tilted back her head, and opened her mouth to kiss him back with such an eagerness that he groaned deep in his throat. Somehow they ended up on the bed, and he ended up on top of her, and their clothes ended up on the floor. His weight was so delicious and erotic, and her need so intense, that there was no time for gentleness or the luxury of leisurely lovemaking.

Some time later Jessica was searching around for her clothes, which were strewn all over the floor, and Damien was belting his jeans when they both distinctly heard the front door slam.

Her hand flew up to her mouth in horror, and her eyes flew to his in consternation. 'Dad? Here—so early?' And suddenly she was scrabbling into her clothes as fast as she could, in record time, and brushing her hair furiously away from her face. Damien's mouth twitched at the corners as he watched her fly, and he then went to the door to unlock it and walk out on to the landing. She joined him, cheeks very flushed, as footsteps sounded out to the kitchen. Then she moaned, 'Lunch! I totally forgot that Dad was coming home for lunch!'

'Anybody there?' Will's voice echoed through the house. 'I'm home. Is lunch going to be late?'

Jessica made an odd sort of squeaking noise as Damien strolled unconcernedly to the top of the stairs and descended. At a loss as to what to do next, she followed reluctantly, and Will's bushy white brows shot up very high as he saw them both coming from the first floor, his daughter's colour very high indeed and Damien's hair more ruffled than he had ever seen it.

'Dad!' she exclaimed intelligently, jumping violently when Damien put a deliberate arm around her at the bottom of the stairs. She pushed vainly with one arm against his side, but he refused to let go, and this made her face flame even more with embarrassment. She had never got around to telling her father the exact nature of her relationship with Damien because she had never really been sure how he would take it, and the fact that both men were watching her flush so closely made her flush even more. 'We were, he was, I——'

'What your daughter is so eloquently trying to tell you is that she has agreed to marry me,' Damien interrupted smoothly, 'and preferably as soon as possible. Darling, I didn't know that you could blush like that! I've never seen your colour so high!'

Her poise completely gone with that, she resorted to a furious, 'Shut up!' as she tried to hide her cheeks with her hands. He grabbed them and forced her fingers away from her cheeks as he laughed down at her face.

Will said mildly, 'I guess it does mean that lunch will be late, after all.'

The next morning, Jessica swore disgustedly as she tore off the second pair of tights that had run when she'd tried to put them on. She felt sure that the world was against her and had been against her from the very moment she had opened her eyes. She had got out of bed and had promptly tripped on the upturned corner of the rug, falling and bruising her knee painfully. Then, finding herself late, she had burned herself with her curling iron, knocked her favourite bottle of perfume on the floor, making the room reek horribly, so she had to open up the window for fresh air while she finished dressing. The weather was very cold outside and the room felt like a freezer.

She threw her ruined tights across the room and swore roundly for a few more minutes. Then, in a much cheerier frame of mind, she drew off her skirt and pulled on a pair of slacks instead. Soon completely dressed, she hurried to limp downstairs to be greeted by the sight of Damien, already dressed and waiting for her, his foot tapping impatiently. He hated it when people were late. 'You've finally made it, I see,' he said shortly. 'Sit down and I'll pour you a cup of coffee. We need to leave in a few minutes if we're going to make it to New York by the afternoon.' They had decided to hurry back to start the wedding preparations as soon as possible, both opting for a very quiet ceremony with only witnesses and Jessica's father in attendance.

'I know just exactly what time it is,' she snapped irritably back, as she pulled out a chair and sank into it, her hand going to rub the sore knee. 'And I don't need you hovering about to remind me.'

His eyebrows shot up at that as he walked over and poured her the hot liquid promised, bringing the mug to sit it in front of her. 'Chipper mood we're in today, I can see,' he replied sarcastically, and she scowled at him from over the rim of the mug.

'You may be chipper,' she muttered sourly, 'but I'm not, so don't make any more thoughtless generalisations than you can help, hmm? This coffee's too strong.' She pushed away the mug in disgust.

'The coffee's exactly how it's been made several times before,' Damien returned evenly, his brow beginning to lower forbiddingly, 'and you've drunk it without complaining. Now I suggest that you either finish that cup or get back upstairs and finish packing so that we can get out of here, instead of sitting there and looking foul.'

'My things are already packed,' she said sweetly, and she sat back to cross her legs deliberately.

He gave her a warning look that said clearly, 'Watch it!' There was some bafflement too at her hostile behaviour, but all he said was, 'Then I had better go and get your suitcases while you drink your coffee.'

'I don't want my coffee.'

A deep breath from him, pent up. 'Then why don't you come up with me and carry down one of the lighter cases?'

'I banged my knee.'

'Then sit right where you are, for God's sake!'

'I want to go and say goodbye to Dad.'

'Jessica Alaina King!' It was not just a shout; it was a roar that shook the windows. 'You get your rear end out that door and to the car this instant and sit there, don't do or say anything but just sit there until I get out with your things so we can go!' Her eyebrow went up, her mouth pursed dangerously, and he saw the warning signs of a full-fledged outburst of temper brewing in her. She knew that he saw it, for she noticed his eyes flicker and change, but he still shook a stiff finger at her, too angry himself now at her provoking behaviour to really change his attitude. 'Go on, move it!'

She stood, bowed slightly in a mocking way, one hand sketching an obeisance, and then exited with a dignified limp. Once out of the house, though, she stood tapping one angry, frustrated foot while she looked daggers at the mailbox by the end of the driveway. She had wanted to goad Damien into losing his temper and had been spoiling for a fight ever since she had come down the stairs, but irrationally, now that she had got him good and angry, she felt more frustrated than ever instead of satisfied. She felt like lashing out at anyone or anything that happened to come into her orbit; she felt like crying out the tears that had not come with the strange flat depression last night; she felt like smashing her fist on something nicely solid. She wanted to plant a right hook on Damien's jaw, that's what she wanted to do.

Why had she ever agreed to marry him in the first place? She had to be the biggest fool in the world to tie herself to him like that. She despised herself for her weakness, for giving in and putting up with whatever he would give her, and yet she couldn't back out. She felt caught, trapped by her own feelings for him, and that made her furious. She knew that it was a false hope to expect him to one day return any love she now felt for him. If it hadn't happened in the last three years, then it wouldn't happen at all. Everything was too late. Damien was hanging on to a past emotional need and ruined relationship, and she was doing the same thing, trying to go back. It was all so futile.

She'd had such high ideals and purposes when she had first come back home! And all he had to do was to waltz right into her life, and everything settled and fixed in her mind went topsy-turvy, jumbling up and then falling into an altogetherly new picture. Her eyes went back to the house behind her, narrowing and amazingly cat-like in their slant. Then with her mind made up, she swung around briskly to take off down the street.

Her father's bookstore was just a few blocks away, and though she had said goodnight and goodbye to him the night before, she thought that she would pop in for a minute to give him one more hug. It would make Damien absolutely livid.

The bell jangled cheerfully as Jessica pushed open the front door. She controlled the impulse to turn around and yank the little sleigh bells right out of the wall, and she smiled brightly at her father's look of surprise. There were a few customers milling around already, even though it was still fairly early in the morning.

Will said mildly, 'Why, this is a surprise! I thought that you and Damien would be halfway to New York by now!'

She laughed at that and inwardly winced at the false sound. Her father didn't seem to notice anything amiss.

'We're only half an hour late, Dad! There's no need to exaggerate! I just thought I'd come over and give you another hug before we took off.' She slipped around to the back of the counter and just then one of the customers came up with a few cards and a paperback novel.

Her father rang up the purchases and took the proffered cash, chatting with the lady who was a regular in the store. Jessica knew her by sight and passed a few comments back and forth with her, watching the front door with one eye. Sure enough, in just about the time she had expected, a sleek black car slid to a stop just outside the shop. It was Damien's car, she saw with a grim amusement. She bent suddenly on the pretence of tying her shoelace, slightly appalled at the imp of mischief that was prompting her to go on when common sense should have told her to stop.

The little bells jangled and footsteps approached the counter. 'Hello, Will,' came Damien's voice, pleasant and unruffled. She stifled a snort. He would be just about red hot now, and ready to explode. 'Have you seen Jessica anywhere? I seem to have misplaced her.'

She rose slowly to her full height, meeting his dark snapping eyes and hard smile as her father said, 'She's just tying her shoe here, and ready to go. She wanted to hop over and give me a quick hug before you two left.' He sent a quick, slightly puzzled glance over to Jessica, sensing something between the two but not sure what.

Jessica let her eyes slide away from Damien, stubbornly ignoring the stern unspoken message he was communicating to her. She turned to her father and started to speak. 'We'll get in touch with you, probably within the next few days, Dad, to let you know when you should get someone to look after the shop, okay? Is there anything else we need to discuss?'

Will smiled at her fondly. 'If so, we can discuss it on the phone later, dear. It was nice of you to drop by.'

'Well,' she said brightly, 'I guess we'd better get going——' Someone else walked up with a few purchases, and she stepped nimbly back, just out of Damien's reach. '——Oh, please do go on ahead,' she invited the customer politely, returning Damien's glare with a blank one of her own.

Will rang up the purchases quickly enough, and Jessica's eyes wandered around the shop idly while he did so. Her gaze came to the corner in the store that was exclusively for bridal paraphernalia, a popular corner since June, the traditional month for weddings, was nearing. Traditional. Her mind savoured the word with a delicate sarcasm, her eyes going strangely sad. Once she had cherished such wonderful dreams of her own wedding. Now that, too, was gone. She wouldn't have minded a small legal ceremony even then, if there had been just one word of love from Damien. She doubted if she would ever hear it from him. She knew that she should stop the crazy, irrational, irrepressible hope that some day he might just tell her he loved her, but she couldn't seem to make the longing and hope of hearing it die. And of course the waiting and the need to hear him admit to love was beginning to bring back all of the old frustrations and tensions that had never really left her. Some day the false expectations will die, she knew tiredly. But why did it have to take so long for her? Youth, she thought, is a sad thing to grow out of, when you can feel the dreams fade away.

'. . . Honey?' her father was saying gently, and her eyes came back into focus. Her eyes winged to Damien's involuntarily and found him staring at her with the oddest expression on his face, contemplative, gentle. Damien being gentle this morning, after how she had goaded him? She shook her head quickly and decided she was being fanciful, as she turned to give her father a warm and affectionate hug. Then she and Damien were saying goodbye once again and heading out the door.

Damien was in a silent mood, as they pulled away from the kerb, scant moments later. He must still be angry, she surmised, and she really couldn't blame him, not after the unpardonable way she had behaved. His mood suited hers, for she had never really shaken the depression from the night before, and she put her head back on the head rest and closed her eyes. Damien left her alone and they travelled for quite some time in silence.

She dozed lightly, having spent a restless night, and then roused as the car slowed and the sound of the engine changed. Opening her eyes and looking around, she said suddenly, 'Oh, Damien, slow down a minute, will you? Would you pull over, quickly?'

Reacting with a smooth swiftness that she briefly admired, he had the car off the road and slowing to a stop. He looked at her with a frown, saying, 'What's the matter, are you feeling ill?'

'Oh, no.' She opened her door and scrambled out and he quickly followed, his frown of concern changing to one of puzzlement and incomprehension.

'Then why did you want to stop, for heaven's sake?' She was watching both sides of the road, preoccupied, and as an opening appeared in the traffic, she ran across and he again followed. 'Jessica, what's the matter?'

'Nothing, I told you. I just wanted to look down this embankment, that's all.' It was, if she was not mistaken, the scene of her accident. She hadn't noticed before, being too tired to look around when her father had driven her home from the hospital. She was right; over to the left was a pair of deep indentations about the width of a car's tyres, and down on the ground at the bottom of the hill was the scar still left from her rolling car. She pointed down to it and he turned his head to look. 'See that? That's where my car rolled. I hadn't realised that the embankment was so steep—no wonder my car was a total write off!'

'My God!' Damien paled as he surveyed the distance down to the bottom. 'The car must have rolled about three or four times, at least!'

'The police said about four and a half,' she said casually, losing interest and walking away now that she had seen in daylight what had been at night-time a surrealistic, terrifying experience. 'It landed on the driver's side, and I had luggage, pencils, and the map thrown all over me. What a night!'

The road was again clear and she ran lightly across, looking curiously back when she sensed that Damien was no longer with her. He still stood motionless, staring down at the ravine for some time. She had begun to feel impatient when he finally turned and walked slowly back.

After climbing back into the car, he asked her abruptly, 'Where was your car towed?'

'It was at a little garage on the other side of town. You can almost see the place from here, and that's a small town! It's probably at the junkyard by now.'

'Do you know where the junkyard is?' He reached out a hand and the car purred to life.

'I think it's not far from the garage,' she said, frowningly. 'At least that's what I heard from one of the attendants at the garage. Why do you ask?'

'We're going there.' He revved the engine and pulled out on to the street. Jessica not only felt puzzled at that, but she felt irritated too. He was the one who had wanted to get going this nmorning, and now he wanted to waste time!

'I don't see the point,' she argued. 'We're just wasting time, and you were the one that wanted to get to New York in such a hurry this morning.'

'So? I've changed my mind,' he replied shortly, slewing to a stop at the small garage that she pointed out. She sighed with impatience as he got out of the car and approached one of the uniformed attendants. After a few moments of conversation, he was back in the car, reversing, and taking a nearby side road.

At the small and untidy junkyard Jessica easily spotted and pointed out for Damien what was left of her car. He didn't say anything but just stared out the window of the car, his head averted to the mangled wreckage stored there. All she could see of him was the shine of his black silky hair and the edge of one closely shaven jaw. As her eyes touched that edge, she saw a muscle bunch. Something kept her quiet for a few moments, as he continued to stare across the street, his long body tense. Then, with a queer look on his face and widened, dilated eyes, he started the car again to head back to the highway.

She managed to keep quiet for the next mile or so and then, without looking at him, she asked, 'What was that all about?'

He didn't reply at once. 'It's a miracle that you lived through that at all, let alone coming out with a mere cut on the face.'

She shrugged lightly. 'I guess that's true. I certainly felt lucky at the time. But it's over now, and there's no use harping back to it. Thousands of people live through car smash-ups.'

He muttered something at that, something brief and abrupt that she didn't catch.

Startled, she asked, 'What was that?'

He shook his head, clearing his expression of that strange look. 'Nothing. It's nothing. Just forget it.'

Baffled and impatient, she expelled a short gusty breath. 'That's what I've been trying to say for the last half hour.' All he did was look at her once, his dark eyes unfathomable.

That was the end to their conversation until they stopped for lunch, a few hours later. Jessica felt so strange, talking to Damien with every appearance of normality and seeing other women eye him covetously. His looks attracted a great amount of attention from the opposite sex, for he seemed to dominate the restaurant when he stood to walk with a prowling grace, making the open areas for traffic seem suddenly very small to everyone there. This man was her fiancé. This man was shortly going to take vows with her that he would probably never even mean, doing lip service to a ceremony that promoted a life commitment and a solid relationship.

What would happen, she wondered, as she stared coldly at a man who was eyeing her too vividly, when I begin to fade, losing what looks I have? What will happen if he ever gets tired of me? Damien noticed the man staring at her and gave him a wide-eyed, icy look that sent him back to his newspaper with great rapidity.

Something inside seemed to panic briefly and she cried inwardly, this is not what I want! I want love and affection and security! Passion and some kind of undefined, vague need just isn't enough! She suddenly, fervently hoped that he would begin to see things the same way also, before they actually were married.

She couldn't lose heart. There was so much to hope for, every sign of a possible successful marriage and life with Damien. She had to have faith in her own strong, private convictions and in his innate personality, that giving, caring man that could surface so briefly and then disappear. Everything could be so much easier if she were looking only for the surface, physical passions, if she could have been content with their past relationship. She felt sure that he would never have offered her marriage then, and she wondered if he would someday resent her for pushing him to the commitment. She sincerely hoped he wouldn't see it that way, for she had been very serious when she'd tried to break off with him completely.

It's just that she couldn't seem to give him up.

She waited patiently while he paid for their lunch, her face turned to the large picture window and the scenery outside. She was so deep into her own contemplations and uncertainties that she didn't notice when he had finished his brief transaction with the cashier. He slowed the hand that he had automatically outstretched to get her attention and just stared at her.

Her slim body was outlined by the afternoon yellow rays shooting into the foyer, gleaming on elegant black slacks and burnished crimson hair that flowed abundantly down to her graceful shoulders. She had on a shimmery peasant blouse that opened wide at the throat to reveal the delicate bone structure there. Gold gleamed at her throat and wrist as she folded her arms casually across her chest. Her face was cameo pure, carved in ivory and painted with delicate porcelain colours. The scar cut a rakish slant across the one brow, no longer angry and red, and the contrast between it and the perfection of her face was startling, eye-riveting, but certainly not repulsive. She merely looked human, no longer the unattainable sex goddess built up by the media, though she was still quite lovely.

Then the spell was broken as she turned her head,

sensing his regard, and she smiled as he came forward immediately. It cut across her face, as keen as a ray of sunshine. 'Are we ready to go?'

He reached out an arm, put it across her shoulders and drew her near, smiling back. 'Yes, we are. Let's leave.'

CHAPTER TEN

NEW York was a bit of a culture shock to her and she laughed a little as she rummaged through her purse for some aspirin to alleviate a headache that was beginning to pound at her temples. 'It's funny how easily one can lose the tolerance for big city noises,' she commented, in response to Damien's sidelong glance. 'This is strangely like a foreign country to me! I don't know, I think I prefer the quieter atmosphere of a small town and a cosy neighbourhood like where Dad lives.'

'You'd like it only for a little while,' she was told amusedly, 'and then you'd be climbing the walls for something exciting to do! You know that you'd never be able to stand that pace for long.'

She had to chuckle at his astute assessment of her. 'You're probably right. But I still have a headache from all that noise!'

He smiled in sympathy and reached out to briefly squeeze her hand, and she knew in that moment why she loved him so much. She knew it as she took in his sensitivity and sometimes quite unexpected understanding, his endearingly disarming smile and his sparkling dark eyes. She knew and never questioned again that she would love him all her life.

And somehow that quietly changed her, right there in the car, stuck smack in the middle of New York traffic. Though she was talking lightly to Damien and making smart remarks that made him laugh, her mind was working on another level, assimilating that inner knowledge and deriving a certain measure of peace and serenity from it. She didn't have to be angry with him, and she didn't have to struggle to restrain a constant element of rage against either him, or herself. She could let it all go. He was himself, and that essence of him that made him what he was, was what she loved so.

It was plain and simple, true love. No matter how he hurt her, no matter who he slept with, no matter if he left her—she loved him and would continue to love him. That's what she had struggled against from the very beginning, that love that made her so vulnerable and open to possible hurt. She was no fool over him. That had been erroneous thinking on her part. Love gave one a kind of dignity and purpose, whether it was an altruistic love of mankind or a personal romantic love, and all types of caring had a common bond of both selflessness and selfishness, and a certain amount of joy and pain. She shouldn't struggle against that. It was a simple, unchangeable fact, and she'd accepted it at last.

She began to sit up and take notice when Damien began to turn down streets that would take them to his neighbourhood instead of to her apartment, which had been the original destination. 'Damien?' she started hesitantly. He didn't seem to hear. 'Aren't we going the wrong way? Did you forget that you were taking me home first so that I could get some things done?'

Slowing the car and turning on to his street, he replied, 'No, I didn't forget that I was taking you home.' Strange wording, that, she thought. He must have meant that he was supposed to take her home. 'But I wanted to talk to you, and thought that you could perhaps postpone whatever you were going to do tonight. Will you stay for supper?'

'Sure. But you know,' she said wryly, as he cut the engine after pulling up the long private drive that led to his elegant home, 'all you had to do was ask. You didn't have to kidnap me.'

'No, I guess I didn't.' He smiled a strange, preoccupied smile, and she leaned over to gently kiss his cheek, feeling his start. He leaned back to look down into her eyes. 'What was that for?'

She touched him on the shoulder and then unbuckled her seat belt. 'Just because I felt like giving you a present,' she teased, 'and I didn't happen to be near a five-and-dime store!'

'So come here and kiss me properly,' he murmured, reaching out a compelling hand. She chuckled and then pressed her lips briefly to his, but opened her door and got out afterwards.

'Now is neither the time nor the place for the kind of embrace that you have in mind, lecher.'

He got out of the car also and leaned against the roof with his arms folded, grinning lazily into her eyes. 'And what do you think I have in mind?'

'There's a stick shift,' she pointed out prosaically. 'How close can you get with a stick shift, for heaven's sake?'

'You have a point there.' He ducked his head to survey the interior of the car thoughtfully. 'Well, that does it.'

'What does what?' she asked in amusement, as she bent her head also and peered at him through the two windows and the interior. His dark eyes danced.

'We'll just have to get a family car,' he said wickedly, a seldom seen dimple appearing in his lean cheek as his grin widened.

She laughed aloud and turned her head to hide a blush. He bounded around and peered into her face with a great delight. 'Hot damn! Two blushes in as many days, I don't believe it!'

'Quit, will you?' she protested, laughing all the harder as she tried to escape from him by running up the steps to the front door. She was doomed to failure as he followed closely, tickling her at the waist in a way that made her wriggle and shriek. At that moment she felt happier than she could remember feeling in years, and by his unspoken but obvious contentment as he put his arm around her waist, she knew that he had to feel something like what she was feeling also.

But she must have been wrong, for his face was changing, the smile in his eyes fading away to leave something dark and troubled behind. From the one laughing moment to the next sober instant he had changed so much that she felt chilled and apprehensive. 'Come on inside,' he said quietly.

She followed him down the main hall after he had greeted Esther, his housekeeper, and she asked him shortly, 'What is it, Damien? What's wrong?'

He didn't answer but continued until he reached the comfortable, roomy den, and he held the door open for her to pass through first. She murmured a polite thanks automatically, and she walked on into the room to turn quickly to face him, waiting for him to speak. And he didn't even then, but walked to the right of the room which held several shelves and cabinets, and he poured them both stiff drinks, handing her one glass. She sat, jerkily, and sipped from the glass with a kind of desperate eagerness that would have told him just how much he was upsetting her, but he didn't see it. He was staring down into his glass, whirling it gently, not drinking. He seemed so far away right then that she doubted if he would have noticed if she'd got up and left.

What did he want to talk about? she wondered. What did he want to say? This was it. He's changed his mind.

He didn't want to get married after all. She shook her head with impatience and puzzlement, and bounded out of her chair to pace around the room like a caged animal. That didn't make sense, not after the affectionate, light-hearted quip he'd made about a family car. Or was it then that he had realised he didn't want a commitment that was as binding as marriage, after all? She came to a stop at a large window and stared out, feeling adrift in a sea of uncertainty. Was she to live like this for the rest of her life, always uncertain, always wondering about him, always afraid? Love didn't cancel out fear, she found, gripping her glass in two sweat-dampened palms.

And then he was speaking quietly. 'And now I think it's about time we had that talk, don't you?' Her hand went out to the heavy, floor-length curtain, grasped it, tightened. 'Jessica.' It was said gently. 'Come away from the window and sit down.'

She turned, jerkily, and faced him from across the room but couldn't seem to get the impetus to carry herself to the chair near him that he was indicating. A host of emotions was paralysing her; dread, the foremost emotion, locked her joints into immobility. All she could do was to face him, her complexion very pale against the background of flame red hair and dark green curtains, and her own vulnerability at the moment was extremely apparent.

His expression changed as he looked at her. 'Jess, what are you afraid of?' he asked gently. 'I'm not going to beat you. Please, come and sit down.'

And so she did, staring at him all the while, waiting for him with a rising impatience and a heightened emotion to speak, to say anything! And as she watched him, her eyes widened as she realised that he too was nervous about something, his shoulders hunched and his eyes wide and vulnerable. She sat straight, not daring to think.

'Oh, my dear,' he half sighed, half moaned. 'I don't know where to begin. I—something happened to me today that I'd like to explain to you.' This was it. She knew it.

She couldn't stand it any longer as he paused yet again as if he were searching for the right words. 'You don't want to get married after all, do you?' she asked jerkily, wrenching her eyes away to stare blindly in the other direction. 'That's it, isn't it? All you have to do is say so, Damien. I won't bind you to me if you want to change your mind.'

'No!' he exclaimed incredulously, and she heard a chink of glass. A split second later, he was pulling her out of the chair and into his arms and holding her so tightly she thought her ribs would break. 'That's not at all what I was going to say! Whatever gave you that idea, darling? Don't you even yet trust me? Can't you have just a little faith in me, for once?'

Her face suddenly crumpled and the tears came so quickly and uncontrollably that they splashed down her cheeks almost before she knew it. 'I'm so afraid to,' she moaned. 'I'm sorry. I'm sorry. . . .' She gave a sob, caught her breath, and subsided into silence, her great swimming eyes regarding him mutely.

His hands came to her face, tenderly, caressingly. 'You don't know even yet, do you, darling?' he whispered. 'You don't dare let yourself know it, do you? Hush, now, it's all right. Listen to me a minute now, without jumping to such hasty conclusions. When I looked down that ravine that you so easily could have died in, I suddenly wondered just why was I holding everything in? What was the point? I guess what I was doing, was wanting to do at least, was waiting until the convenient time and place before telling you just how very much I love you. I didn't want to feel uncomfortable! I didn't want to bare myself that way! I had a host of reasons for not telling you, and I looked down that ravine and realised how stupid they all really were. I—darling, are you hearing all this?' That last was said with a slightly shaky laugh.

Jessica's eyes had glazed over with a stunned disbelief as she heard the words that she'd longed to hear for such an eternity. Her lips were parted and her expression was blank, and everything else that he had said had faded into insignificance after those three magical words. 'What? What did you say?' she murmured distractedly, coming back to the present at his insistent question.

'I was just trying to tell you, my love, that when I really realised how you had nearly died, I suddenly knew that I had to tell you how much I love you, right now, while I still had the chance, and still had you with me,' he said quietly. 'You're shaking like a leaf! Stop it, Jessica, sweetheart. You're making me feel badly for springing it on you like this, and it's not something I particularly want to go on a guilt trip about!'

His arms tightened even more around her as she started to laugh shakily, burying her head in his shirt, her own arms creeping around his lean waist. Happiness was coursing through her giddily, and a sort of intense, overwhelming, long-sought-for relief. And with the relief came a marvellous loosening of the tension that had gripped her for three long years. She relaxed fully against Damien's warm, strong chest, and it was the most wonderful feeling in the world.

'How long have you loved me?' she whispered, muffled in his shirt. She felt his cheek come down on her head, and he rubbed it gently back and forth in the softness of her hair.

'I don't know. Forever, it seems like. At least now when I look back, I can see that I loved you. You said to me once that you appreciated my efforts at being truthful whenever possible, and I felt terrible when I heard you. Not only was I not being entirely truthful with you, but I was not being truthful with myself. I tried everything I knew to blind myself to my own emotions and my need, and I deliberately went away for months at a time to see if I could stay away, and never come back to you. So you see, you didn't drive me away. I drove myself away, and I couldn't admit that to you without admitting that I loved you. I was afraid, afraid of loving too much, I guess, of showing you how I needed you, and knowing myself how much I need you.' His voice trailed away to a whisper and then stopped, and they were both silent for a long time, just holding each other, just being together.

'I'm sure that you know I love you too!' Jessica said, a quiver of laughter, self-mockery, and something else running through her voice. 'When did I give it away?'

'I think I began to suspect that night you became so delightfully drunk,' he murmured, passing his hand through her hair and cupping the back of her slender neck tenderly. 'Or perhaps when you spent so much time and effort on little Mary Coefield, all the while knowing that I could have asked her to marry me. It must have taken a great deal of courage, darling.'

She merely shrugged slightly, rubbing her face against the warmth of his thin cotton shirt, feeling the hard living muscle beneath. He felt so good, so vital and alive, and she loved him so. But then he was loosening his arms and drawing back, and her eyes flew to his face questioningly.

'We have a lot to talk over,' he told her gently, and he drew her down on to the couch. She went obediently and sat looking at him with her large, glowing, loving eyes trained on him. He groaned, reached out for her, and kissed her long and lingeringly.

And this time it was she who leaned back, placing both hands on his shoulders and smiling wryly into his face. 'Can I confess something I probably should have never hidden from you in the first place?' she began, dropping her eyes and beginning to feel and look embarrassed. 'I'm sorry that I didn't tell you at the beginning, but I was a—virgin that first night with you. Now I feel that I've cheated both myself and you because I didn't tell you. That was a special gift, and I shouldn't have been afraid to admit it. It's—it's just that I wanted you so much, and I was afraid that if you knew, you'd back away. It was stupid of me, wasn't it?'

His fingers came up and probed her lips, the tips of them sliding across her lower lip, caressing her lightly. She pursed her lips and kissed him. 'And I have to confess that I knew,' he told her gently, making her eyes fly to his, widened.

'You knew all along?'

'No, I knew afterwards. There were little things, your reaction was untutored, surprised, even though you tried to hide it. It frightened me so much that I nearly ran away right then, but I then convinced myself that you were adult enough to know what you were doing and to take the consequences. It was rationalisation on my part; on the one hand I was terrified of commitment, and on the other hand I was so tied to you already I couldn't have left you alone, no matter how I tried.'

'Poor baby,' she mocked gently, and was rewarded with another devastating kiss. She responded gladly, threading her fingers through his hair and touching his strong jaw line lightly. He pulled her to him, one hand pressed to the small of her back, bringing her whole body against his, and he broke off the kiss to bury his mouth against her neck, biting gently, making her shudder.

'Do you realise,' he whispered, and his moving lips on her neck were a caress, 'how terribly long it's been since we've made love?'

'Mmn,' was her bemused response, as her thoughts winged back to the day before. She smiled. 'Let me see. It seems like forever, doesn't it?'

'Yes, it does. You have to move in right away, so that we don't have to worry about which place we're going to sleep at.' His hands were passing over her rib cage, and she felt his own answering smile on her neck.

'Tell me,' she said suddenly, drawing her head back to look at him searchingly, a trace of uncertainty still lingering in her eyes and mind. 'Do you think that you really could have gone through with marrying Mary?'

He half sighed, half laughed. 'No. It was a last ditch effort of mine to try and shake off your spell, you witch. I was in the last convulsive throes while you relentlessly reeled in the line. I was a fish, hooked by the bait, and you were my captor.'

'Disgusting analogy,' she said complacently, 'and I thought as much, you devil. Well, you've led me a merry dance, but as long as you now know who's the boss, I'll not be too harsh on you.' His hands began to tighten warningly, as his eyes sparkled a laughing challenge.

'We'll . . . er, wrestle that one out later,' he promised, and she muffled a laugh. They certainly would. His eyes grew more serious and he said softly, 'I just want to say a few more things, Jessie. The first is that it gave me such a queer, frightening shock to look at the tangled wreckage of your car earlier today, and everything else dimmed in comparison. The past was really past at that moment for me, and it didn't matter any more for the first time in years. It really didn't matter, and I realised that it hadn't for some years now. All that matters to me now is you and our future together. Everything else is secondary. And I was a fool, for stubbornly believing that women are not to be trusted, and are not dependable. It was irrational and beneath me to classify you in the same category with women like my mother. Anyone can see that you're poles apart! I was just trying to avoid getting hurt.' She went forward, the happiness in her making her eyes glow more than ever, and she kissed him softly, thankfully, on the mouth.

Impulsively, she asked. 'Damien, what if your mother were to walk through your front door one day? What would you do?' As he hesitated, her eyes searched his for any remnant of pain. There was none.

'Who knows?' he shrugged frankly. 'I might kick her out right away. If she were pitiful enough, I might write her a cheque and then kick her out. I can't really see her coming all the way from Chicago, if that's where she still lives, just to find out if I'm alive and around, so I guess the question is not really applicable.' Jessica felt sad at that, sad that such a woman even existed, let alone the fact that no one could really love her. And she felt sad that Damien had been starved early in life of the kind of affection and security that everyone needs. She could understand him so much better now, and she couldn't believe that she hadn't seen before the vulnerability underneath his strength. She would probably never be able to look at him again without thinking of his splendid struggle to overcome the environment that he had been born in, and his single-minded determination to rise above the obstacles that fate had thrown in his way. She had felt proud of herself and the achievements she'd accomplished in her own profession by sheer ability and hard work, but in comparison to Damien's struggle, hers now seemed pitifully weak.

But the ghost of the past faded away as Damien pulled her around and on top of his lap and said with satisfaction, 'Jessica Kent has a nice ring to it, doesn't it?'

'Oh, I don't know,' she replied offhandedly, and was treated with a wary, stern look. She chuckled. 'I rather like the sound of Damien King, myself.'

'Oh, you do, do you?' he growled, pulling at her shoulders so that she collapsed on his chest and had to stare at him from a distance of about an inch away. 'Jessie, there's the second thing I almost forgot.'

She mischievously sent an exploring, tickling finger into the space between his shirt buttons, low down on his stomach, and she laughed at his jump. 'Oh, and what's that?'

'Stop that!' he ordered, laughter breaking up the stern command in his voice. 'This is serious, now!'

'I thought we had managed to cover just about everything,' she complained, as he grabbed at her fingers. 'Isn't it time for a little play now?'

'In a minute.' He grabbed her other marauding hand and frowned into her eyes and then smiled, and the open, tender look of love was so welcome, so eagerly awaited by her that she subsided, not to hear what he had to say but just to drink in that look. 'I just wanted to tell you, darling,' he whispered, bringing his hands up to cup her face, 'that you are the most beautiful woman in the world to me, and always will be. I never want you to change because I love you just the way you are.'

Her hand automatically went up to the scar on her

brow, her eyes questioning, and he nodded. 'You misunderstood me that night, darling. I was upset because you had been hurt and could have been killed, not because you were scarred.' She smiled brilliantly at him, feeling so much joy that she thought she might burst from it, and he cocked his head to the side as he considered her appraisingly. 'Besides, I rather like it. It gives you an air of mystery and romantic intrigue.' And he watched her, amused and puzzled, as she threw back her head to laugh heartily.

CHAPTER ELEVEN

'JUSTIN, my love, the man is an incorrigible flirt,' Jessica said calmly, sipping tea. They both looked over to Damien, who stood with his black head bent towards an incredibly tiny, wizened old lady with a great mass of white, white hair, and he was turning on the charm as only he knew how to do. They both registered the old lady's simper and girlish pat to Damien's arm.

'Quite hopeless,' Justin agreed placidly, settling his teacup back in its saucer. The two sat in chairs pulled around to face a little side table which held their cups and saucers, and two empty dessert plates. They surveyed and commented on the crowd of people that milled about the huge, open room, at ease with each other as only old friends can be. Mrs Coefield had really outdone herself with all the decorations and the refreshments, on top of the huge and elegant dinner they had just enjoyed. She had overdone it, Jessica thought privately, but the woman after all only had one daughter to marry off, and hopefully this would be the only engagement party that Mary ever threw.

'Oh, look, darling, over there at the two young love-birds opening their engagement presents,' Jessica said, boredom dripping from her voice as she nodded to her right. Justin turned his head briefly and then looked back at her.

Laughter shook his voice as he said, 'My dear, heaven help you if you should ever run out of social acts to play out! Anyone would think you were a world-weary, disillusioned wife who had seen all of the joys and sorrows that marriage and life could bring you, when instead you've only been married two months, yourself! Come on now, confess! You feel very sentimental about those two over there since you were the one who introduced them, don't you?'

'Well,' she said thoughtfully, her head cocked to one side and her eyes twinkling merrily, 'just a twinge perhaps! But don't you tell a soul, Justin Marsh! I've my reputation to think of. Now, just look at that scoundrel of a husband, will you? He's flirting with *three* old ladies! Where does he find them?'

'God only knows.' Justin shook his blond head. 'I never thought I'd see the day when I would say this, but Jessica, I must admit that I think I like that guy!'

She gurgled a laughing response and Justin took his time perusing her smiling profile. Sleek, sophisticatedly attired as always, and radiantly beautiful, she had an air of contentment that he had never seen before. Slim legs crossed at the knee, and tiny straps of leather adorned her graceful feet. She wore basic black, a filmy transparent wisp of a dress over a strapless black slip. A great emerald winked on her left hand, right next to the plain band of gold, and emeralds peeped from both ears from time to time when her hair was swept back enough to allow a glimpse. In the black, she glowed and sparkled with vivid colour, her flaming hair glinting in the light and her eyes golden bright. The one thing marring the absolute perfection of her pure face was the wicked slashing scar over her right brow.

She turned her head and caught his gaze. 'My slip showing?' she asked sweetly, and he had to laugh.

'You know damn well it is, and a sexier slip I've yet to see,' was his return. She wrinkled her nose at him. 'No, I was just thinking that marriage really suits you. You've mellowed out, my dear. I can't sense any repression in you, and you haven't once lost your temper that I know of. You really are happy, aren't you?'

'Wonderfully so,' she said quietly, her eyes winging back to her husband, who was just coming their way. She raised her voice intentionally. 'And no, Justin, I never lose my temper anymore—the only one around our house with a vile disposition is Damien—oh! Hello, darling.'

Damien stood just by Justin's chair, his dark eyes sparkling with laughter. 'Who was the one that broke a vase and a figurine a couple of weeks ago when she found out she wasn't invited to go with me to France?' he asked wickedly. 'Who was the one that ripped up at a fellow, just because he painted her car a different colour than was specified? Who was the one that——'

'That "different colour" was a putrid, stomach turning green,' she responded acidly, 'instead of the maroon clearly indicated on the receipts he'd mixed up, and the vase and figurine was an accident. I was standing closer to them than I had realised when my arm flew out, I told you. Besides, I still think I could have gone with you to France.'

Damien told Justin resignedly, 'An overnight stay at a gloomy old mansion with balding men talking of nothing but business, and she wanted to go!'

'I said "could have" gone with you, not that I would have!' she started heatedly. 'You know perfectly well that——' A sweetly sugared feminine voice came from behind Jessica and she broke off, schooling her expression to one of perfect politeness after the first grimace of distaste. Justin sobered his smile quickly while Damien started to frown forbiddingly.

'Well, well,' the feminine voice cooed, and a slim young woman came around to Jessica's line of vision.

'Is there trouble in this young couple's married paradise already? Hello, Jessica.'

She nodded shortly. 'Hello, Caroline.' Caroline was a model also and had in the past been jealous of Jessica's success and high standing in the profession. Jessica didn't like her much, and neither did the other two men.

'But you know, Damien,' Caroline said sweetly, 'that Jessica must be feeling a bit—tied down, now that she's no longer working because of her disfigurement.'

Justin, Damien and Jessica all regarded each other blankly. Jessica couldn't believe that the other girl could actually have the effrontery to say such a thing in public, and it held her immobile for a moment. Then she heard Justin ask in a confused voice, 'Disfigurement? What disfigurement?'

It was Caroline's turn to look blank as she glanced from one to the other of the trio. 'You know, the scar,' she explained callously.

Jessica had started to smile at Justin's quick response, in spite of her smouldering anger at the other girl's rude insensitivity, and when she heard this, her one mobile brow shot up high, and sparks began to flicker in her diamond bright eyes. She opened her mouth to make a cutting remark when Damien's voice reached her ears, as blank as Justin's had been. 'Scar?' he asked. 'What scar?'

Justin, who had been taking a drink of tea, choked a bit, and Jessica started to shake with a helpless laughter as Caroline, with a swish of her blonde hair, turned and walked away. Justin was laughing then too, as he wiped his mouth with a napkin but Damien looked positively thunderous as he stared at the back of the departing girl.

'I could kick her right in the——' he began.

'Hush, hush, hush,' Jessica said, still laughing. 'Do you really think it matters? Let it go!'

He looked at her. 'It may not matter to you, and I'm glad of that, but it matters to me when someone is so hatefully rude to you.' He then made an obvious effort to relax, she could see, but his eyes still snapped.

'A champion to my cause,' she said to Justin, looking lovingly at Damien. He smiled back, so concerned and caring and wonderfully tender that it made her heart swell full of emotion. She exploded it all into a quick laugh as Damien turned to Justin's seated figure and clapped a hand to his shoulder. He jumped, sending her a wary, startled look, for he had not yet got used to Damien's recent relaxed acceptance of him, even though he had dined at their house and was a frequent and welcome visitor.

'So tell me, Marsh,' said Damien easily. 'Do you like golf?'

Yours FREE, with a home subscription to HARLEQUIN SUPERROMANCE.™

Now you never have to miss reading the newest HARLEQUIN SUPERROMANCES... because they'll be delivered right to your door.

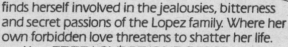

Start with your **FREE** LOVE BEYOND DESIRE. You'll be enthralled by this powerful love story...from the moment Robin meets the dark, handsome Carlos and finds herself involved in the jealousies, bitterness and secret passions of the Lopez family. Where her own forbidden love threatens to shatter her life.

Your **FREE** LOVE BEYOND DESIRE is only the beginning. A subscription to HARLEQUIN SUPERROMANCE lets you look forward to a long love affair. Month after month, you'll receive four love stories of heroic dimension. Novels that will involve you in spellbinding intrigue, forbidden love and fiery passions.

You'll begin this series of sensuous, exciting contemporary novels...written by some of the top romance novelists of the day...with four every month.

And this big value...each novel, almost 400 pages of compelling reading...is yours for only $2.50 a book. Hours of entertainment every month for so little. Far less than a first-run movie or pay-TV. Newly published novels, with beautifully illustrated covers, filled with page after page of delicious escape into a world of romantic love...delivered right to your home.

Begin a long love affair with

HARLEQUIN
SUPERROMANCE.™·

Accept LOVE BEYOND DESIRE **FREE.**

Complete and mail the coupon below today!

- -

FREE! Mail to: Harlequin Reader Service

In the U.S.
2504 West Southern Avenue
Tempe, AZ 85282

In Canada
P.O. Box 2800, Postal Station "A"
5170 Yonge St., Willowdale, Ont. M2N 5T5

YES, please send me FREE and without any obligation my
HARLEQUIN SUPERROMANCE novel, LOVE BEYOND DESIRE. If you do
not hear from me after I have examined my FREE book, please send me
the 4 new **HARLEQUIN SUPERROMANCE** books every month as soon
as they come off the press. I understand that I will be billed only $2.50 for
each book (total $10.00). There are no shipping and handling or any
other hidden charges. There is no minimum number of books that I have
to purchase. In fact, I may cancel this arrangement at any time.
LOVE BEYOND DESIRE is mine to keep as a FREE gift, even if I do not
buy any additional books.   134-BPS-KAPS

NAME _____ (Please Print)

ADDRESS _____ APT. NO.

CITY _____

STATE/PROV. _____ ZIP/POSTAL CODE

SIGNATURE (If under 18, parent or guardian must sign.)

SUP-SUB-22

This offer is limited to one order per household and not valid to present
subscribers. Prices subject to change without notice.
Offer expires March 31, 1985